The Courtship
Maneuver

The Courtship Maneuver

THE COMPLETE SERIES

ALEXA WILDER

The Courtship Maneuver, The Complete Series
Copyright © 2015 by Alexa Wilder
All rights reserved.

No part of this book may be reproduced in any form or by any electronic or mechanical means including information storage and retrieval systems, without permission in writing from the author. The only exception is by a reviewer, who may quote short excerpts in a review.

This book is a work of fiction. Names, characters, places, and incidents either are products of the author's imagination or are used ctitiously. Any resemblance to actual persons, living or dead, events, or locales is entirely co-incidental.

Find out more about the author and upcoming books online at **www.alexawilder.com**

Also by Alexa Wilder

Don't Miss Out on New Releases, Free Stories and More!!

Join Alexa's Readers Group!

AlexaWilder.com/readers-group/

Visit Alexa on Facebook:

Facebook.com/AuthorAlexaWilder

The Wedding Rescue

The Courtship Maneuver

The Stubborn Suitor

The Reckless Secret

The Temptation Trap

The Surprising Catch

Chloe Henson is in love with her boss.

Completely, totally, head over heels in love. She knows he doesn't feel the same way - she doesn't expect him too. Sam Logan is successful and wealthy, and he only dates supermodels. When he could have any woman in Las Vegas, why would he want his shy, abundantly curvy assistant? Determined to ignore her heart, Chloe puts her feelings on hold. But when her brother disappears, and she ends up in the cross-hairs of the Russian mob, she has nowhere to turn. Except to Sam.

Sam Logan has a problem.

He has a thing for his assistant, but he knows he can't act on it. Chloe's the best assistant he's ever had, and over the three years they've worked together, she's become his best friend. Chloe is so shy, he knows one wrong move will send her running. When her irresponsible brother rips off a mob boss and vanishes, Chloe is in danger, and Sam's tired of waiting to make his move. The best way to keep her safe is to make her his. But with bullets flying and betrayal around every corner, can Sam convince Chloe that this is more than just a fling?

CONTENTS

THE COURTSHIP MANEUVER BOOK ONE 1
CHAPTER ONE 3
CHAPTER TWO 12
CHAPTER THREE 17
CHAPTER FOUR 24
CHAPTER FIVE 36
CHAPTER SIX 41
CHAPTER SEVEN 51
CHAPTER EIGHT 58
CHAPTER NINE 69
CHAPTER TEN 77
CHAPTER ELEVEN 83
CHAPTER TWELVE 89
CHAPTER THIRTEEN 95
THE COURTSHIP MANEUVER BOOK TWO 103
CHAPTER ONE 105
CHAPTER TWO 109
CHAPTER THREE 115
CHAPTER FOUR 124
CHAPTER FIVE 131
CHAPTER SIX 139
CHAPTER SEVEN 145
CHAPTER EIGHT 151
CHAPTER NINE 160

CHAPTER TEN	169
CHAPTER ELEVEN	178
CHAPTER TWELVE	187
THE COURTSHIP MANEUVER BOOK THREE	197
CHAPTER ONE	199
CHAPTER TWO	204
CHAPTER THREE	212
CHAPTER FOUR	219
CHAPTER FIVE	223
CHAPTER SIX	233
CHAPTER SEVEN	243
CHAPTER EIGHT	249
CHAPTER NINE	260
CHAPTER TEN	267
CHAPTER ELEVEN	277
EPILOGUE	283
THANK YOU	289
SNEAK PEAK: THE TEMPTATION TRAP	295

the Courtship Maneuver

BOOK ONE

CHAPTER ONE
Chloe

I lay on the couch reading a book on my tablet; the screen dimmed so the light wouldn't give me away. Beside me, a mug of tea steamed, scenting the air with herbs and flowers. I was trying to relax. Tea, a good book, sacking out on the couch. I should have been totally chilled.

Instead, every muscle in my body was tense. The house was brand new, but each creak sent shivers down my spine. I wasn't supposed to be here. No one was. I'd left the lights off, sneaking around in the shadows to set up my sleeping bag on the couch and brewing my tea using the built-in hot water spout in the kitchen. Dinner had been a drive-through burger and fries, the now empty bag sitting on the floor beside me.

The idea had been to hide out, try to calm down somewhere safe, and then figure out what to do. So far, it wasn't working. I'd taken care of the hiding out somewhere safe part. At least I hoped I had. No one who might be looking for me would be looking here.

As far as figuring out what to do? I had no clue. It wasn't even my mess I was running from. It was my baby brother's. I'd been taking care of him our whole lives. It had been suggested to me, more than once, that maybe it was time to stop. But he was my brother. My only real family. I wouldn't turn my back on him.

The glare of headlights flashed across the front windows of the two story house, sending terror crashing through me. No one should be here. There weren't any residents in this neighborhood. It was a new construction community, and I was squatting in the model home.

A truck pulled into the driveway and idled. Struggling to catch my breath, I slid off the couch and moved to hide behind its bulk. Should I try to sneak out the back door? I'd parked a few streets away so my car in the drive wouldn't be obvious, and I'd have to pick my way across the construction site in the dark. But that was preferable to facing the people looking for me.

Suddenly my bright idea about hiding in the model home didn't seem like such a good plan. I was completely isolated, surrounded by acres of mud and silent construction vehicles. No one to hear me scream. No one to help.

The silence of the truck shutting off, followed by the heavy thunk of a door closing had my heart thundering in my chest. What to do? I crab walked backwards into the kitchen and slid across the hardwood floor to hide behind the island. The houses here all had open floor plans. Attractive and practical unless you were trying to hide.

I lost the chance to make a run for the bedrooms when the front door swung open and the lights flipped on. Whoever was here had a key, then. That improved my chances a lot. At the realization of who it must be, my heart calmed, then sank.

Taking a risk, I peaked out around the side of the kitchen island to see who was at the front door. In the glare of the lights I saw a tall figure with broad shoulders, long legs, a lean waist, and a familiar shock of messy blond hair. Sam. Before I could stand up to reveal myself, he spoke.

"I already called the police, so I suggest you get your ass out here and explain yourself before you get arrested."

I jumped to my feet, wishing with all my heart that I wasn't wearing my now very wrinkled suit. It was bad enough that Sam was way out of my league. He didn't need to see me looking like I'd been sleeping in my work clothes.

"Sam, it's me. Don't call the police."

"Chloe?" he said in surprise. Belatedly I noticed he held a gun at his side, his arm tense and ready. He lifted the gun and did something to it before he shoved it in his waistband behind his back. "What the hell, Chloe? I could have shot you."

"I didn't know you had a gun," I said. Not really the point. And kind of a dumb thing to say, but my head was spinning. For a moment, while he was holding that gun, he hadn't looked like my Sam at all. He'd been menacing. Scary.

"Yeah, I have a gun," he said. "And I didn't call the cops. I called Axel. Hold on a sec. And don't move," he barked when I turned to go back to the couch.

He was angry. I couldn't remember the last time I'd seen Sam angry. At least not at me. Sam never got mad at me. Not wanting to piss him off further, I stayed where I was, between the kitchen and the living room, and watched him make a call.

"It's me," he said, scowling in my direction. "Don't worry about it. It was Chloe." A pause. "I have no idea, but I'm going to find out. Yeah, later."

Shoving the phone in his pocket, he pointed to the couch and said, "Sit." I did.

"Did you forget that I had an alarm put on the gate and the spec houses after we had those problems with vandalism last month?" he asked.

Damn it. I had forgotten. Normally, as Sam's assistant, I would have set up something like that, but one of Sam's best friends was Axel Sinclair, who ran the western division of Sinclair Security. Sam had taken care of the arrangements himself. And since I was rarely on site without Sam, it had slipped my mind. Deciding to keep my mouth shut for the moment, I said nothing.

"What are you doing here? Why aren't you at your apartment? What happened? Chloe, are you alright?"

At the open concern in his last question, I burst into tears. I could have held out against anger, but I had no defenses against worry. Not from Sam. I clapped my hands to my eyes trying to stem the flow of tears and calm my hitching breaths when I heard him swear and get up. A moment later he was sitting beside me, pulling me into his arms.

My head fell against his chest and I melted, giving up for the moment on trying to be strong. Sam was here. As long as Sam was here, I was safe. At least for right now.

I'd been Sam Logan's assistant for three years and had been head over heels in love with him for almost all of them.

Sam was smart. Handsome in a way that meant he looked equally good dressed for the construction site as he did in a suit. And he couldn't have been less interested in me. He was a great boss. A good friend. And I knew he cared about me. He had to, otherwise why would he be sitting here letting me cry all over him? But he'd never love me.

I knew that. I'd watched him date a succession of tall, slender, dramatically beautiful women over the years in a series of casually monogamous relationships. And having seen every one of his girlfriends up close at one time or another, I knew why he'd never look at me.

I was a nice person. I was loyal, caring, and fun. But I wasn't tall, skinny, or beautiful. I guessed I was pretty enough. I'd had a few boyfriends who seemed to think so.

My hair and my skin were my best features. My skin was smooth and almost pore less. I'd tell you what moisturizer I use, but it wouldn't help since it's been this way my whole life, no matter what I put on it. And while my hair was a boring light brown, it was shiny, with curl and body. The rest of me was a bit of a let down. If I was feeling generous, I'd call myself curvy. Very curvy. Most days I just felt plump. And I was kind of short. If you picture the opposite of Sam's tall, slender, model girlfriends, you'd get me.

So we were friends, but that was all we'd ever be. Most days I was okay with that. I really hadn't dated much in the past two years, once I finally admitted to myself how I felt about Sam, because every other man just didn't measure up. Right then, terrified and tucked safely into Sam's arms, I wasn't regretting that he'd never love me. I was just grateful he was there.

When I'd run from the back patio of my apartment and snuck to where I'd parked my car on the street, I'd considered going to Sam. But I'd thought he'd said he'd be out tonight. And I didn't want to tell him what was going on until I had a chance to think it through myself. Too late for that now.

My tears gradually faded, and I forced myself to pull away from the heat of Sam's arms. He smelled like spice and citrus. Masculine and strong. Sexy. I wiped at my face and told myself to focus. Yes, Sam is hot. I know that. I see him every day, and every day he's hot. It was not the time to get distracted by how good he looked. And smelled.

Trying to get a little distance, I stood and moved to sit in the arm chair facing the couch. Sam scowled at me again.

"Tell me what's going on Chloe. Now," he said, clearly out of patience.

"Nolan is missing," I admitted. "He didn't come home Saturday night, and he's not answering his phone. I thought maybe he was just-"

"Being typically irresponsible?" Sam said in a dry tone.

Sam wasn't a big fan of my brother. He thought Nolan needed to grow up and stop leaning on me. Sam was probably right. But he didn't understand our relationship. I ignored Sam's comment and went on.

"I got home after work tonight a little later than usual and I had to park a few spots away. I was going in the back because it was closer and I had groceries when I saw people in my apartment. I almost went right in because I thought they might be with Nolan. But then I saw one of them holding a gun."

It had been dizzying, the sway between relief that Nolan was home and shock that there were strangers with weapons in my little apartment.

"I listened to them for a few minutes. They were looking for Nolan. But then they said they wanted to take me in, too."

"Take you in where?" Sam demanded, sitting up straight on the couch.

"I don't know. They had accents, and it was hard to understand what they were saying."

"Did you get a good look at him? At any of them?"

"Not really, I was outside on the patio, trying to stay out of sight behind the blinds. There were three of them. Tall. Dark hair. The one with the gun talked the most."

"What kind of accent?"

"I'm not sure. European. Not French or Spanish. Maybe Russian. Something Eastern European, I think."

"Fuck. Are you sure?"

"No," I said, suddenly annoyed.

I'd done the best I could, but I'd been confused and then scared shitless when they'd said they'd settle for taking me if they couldn't get Nolan. It hadn't occurred to me to stick around and see what else I could find out. I'd turned and run back to my car as quietly as I could, glad I'd left my purse and briefcase in the back seat.

"Sorry, Chloe. I'm just worried. This doesn't sound like one of Nolan's usual fuck-ups."

"No, it doesn't."

Normally I'd bristle at Sam referring to Nolan's occasional issues as 'fuck-ups'. Nolan had made a few mistakes. In the two years he'd been living with me in Vegas, he'd had a DUI and almost lost his license for reckless driving. Helping him with that one had taken a chunk out of my savings. He'd also been fired from two jobs before he'd landed one at the tech start-up where he was currently working. Or had been until a few weeks ago. I'd called Monday morning to find out if he was there, only to hear that he'd been let go almost a month before.

My brother was smart. He was also impulsive and restless. I loved him, but even I could admit it was past time for him to grow up. Before that could happen, I had to find him. Sam pulled his phone back out of his pocket and started to dial. Alarmed, I said,

"Stop, who are you calling?"

"Axel," he said, looking at me as if I was a little slow. Of course he'd be calling Axel.

"You can't call Axel."

"Why not?" Sam asked, starting to look exasperated.

CHAPTER TWO
Chloe

Why not? I knew Axel, at least professionally. Axel was scary. He was very good at his job, the mix-up at the Delecta the month before not withstanding. If I wanted to find Nolan, he'd be the first person to call. But I had a bad feeling about what Nolan might be mixed up in. And if Axel got involved I'd lose control over what was going on. I wanted to protect my brother, even from himself. Axel might not have the same priorities.

"Fine," Sam said, agreeing a little too quickly for me to think he was going to let it go. I worked side by side with the man. I knew that one of his tactics when he wasn't getting his way was to pretend to give up, then come back at the problem from another direction. But I'd play along for now.

"I just need to figure out where he is," I said.

"Forget about your brother for a second," Sam

said. "I want to talk more about the part where they wanted to take you even if they couldn't find him."

"That's all I know," I said. "I pretty much ran right after that."

"That's probably the only smart thing you've done tonight."

"Hey!" I said. I knew I hadn't thought things through as well as I could have, but that was just rude.

"I'm sorry Chloe, but you're an intelligent woman. I've seen your brain in action. And where your dumb-ass brother is concerned, you lose all common sense."

"That's not true." It was. I knew it was. Nolan was my soft spot and my weakness. And if that was so, how much of his current problems were my fault? Maybe if I'd been harder on him… I shut off those thoughts. They weren't going to do me any good until I tracked down my brother.

"It is true," Sam insisted. Standing, he said, "Get your things, we're going home."

"I can't go home, they're looking for me there."

"Not your apartment, my house. You're coming home with me. I have Axel's best security. And I can keep an eye on you while we figure out what to do about Nolan."

"Sam, I appreciate the offer, but I can't come home with you. It's not appropriate. I work for you. What about your Dad?"

It was stupid to protest. I didn't really have anywhere else to go that would be as safe as Sam's house. My best shot had been the model home, but it was clear Sam wouldn't let me stay there. I just didn't think I could deal with the intimacy of being in Sam's house. Living with him. Seeing him all of the day instead of just most of it.

I knew I was heading for a broken heart, and it got worse every day I stayed and worked for him. I should have left and found another job. One that was just work, with a boss who was only my boss. But I hadn't been able to bring myself to leave Sam. Not yet. If I gave in and stayed in his house, I had a feeling it would only push my feelings to the breaking point faster.

"Chloe, Dad loves you. He won't mind you being there. And it's a huge house. We have plenty of room for you."

"But I don't want anyone at work to think-"

"Chloe, it's my company. We can do whatever we want."

"Maybe you can," I said. "But everyone will say-"

"What, that there's something going on? Chloe, they all know us better than that. You're too professional to get involved with me."

"And you'd never fool around with your secretary," I said. "But people still love to gossip."

"First, you're my executive assistant, not my secretary. Secretary sounds so nineteen-fifties. And second, your safety is more important than office gossip.

We come and go together all the time. No one will think anything of it."

Of course they wouldn't. They'd probably assume I'd sleep with Sam in a heartbeat because who wouldn't? But Sam was right, no one would assume he was sleeping with me. And we did come and go together at all hours. I accompanied him to a lot of his meetings, often early and on site, meaning we'd arrived at the office together more than once.

"Okay," I said, unable to come up with a reasonable argument against his plan. I picked up my half drunk tea, rinsed the cup in the sink, and replaced it in the breakfast tray display set up on the counter. Sam waited by the door, prepared to be patient now that he was getting his way. As we left, he locked the door behind us and said,

"Grab your things from your car. I'll have someone bring it to you tomorrow."

"I can follow you," I started to say. Sam gave a sharp shake of his head.

"No. You have unknown guys with guns looking for you. You aren't out of my sight until we resolve whatever's going on. Do you understand?"

I nodded. Sam was usually an easy going guy. Fun. Relaxed. Not too many people knew he also had a temper. It took a while to blow, but when it did, it wasn't pretty. And I'd been there enough to know that he was getting close to his limit. It surprised me. Sam had been pissed since the moment he'd seen me in the model home, but I was fine. What had him so close to the edge so fast?

CHAPTER THREE
Sam

It was taking everything I had not to drag Chloe to Axel's safe room and lock her up until we could find her idiot of a brother. I should have known Nolan was going to cause Chloe trouble. Or worse trouble than he already had. She thought I didn't know about the money she'd paid for the ticket and lawyer when he got his DUI. Chloe thought I didn't know a lot of things.

I glanced over at her in the seat beside me; her face tired, head tilted to lean against the truck's window. She looked tired and sad. And still the most beautiful woman I'd ever seen. I knew she wouldn't agree. She'd say she was plain. She wasn't as showy as a lot of the women around Vegas, but she was something more.

Chloe was luminous. She glowed. Her smooth, perfect gold skin, her gleaming chestnut hair, her warm brown eyes. I wanted to kill anyone who upset her. There wasn't a word for what I wanted to do to the men who had broken into her home and threatened to take her away.

I drove us home in silence, not trusting myself to speak. I was too pissed at her. She was so careful with everyone else and then careless with her self. She should have called me right away. Or gone straight to Axel. She had his number in her cell. She had all my important numbers. She practically ran my life. At least the business side of it. I would have had her in every part of my life if I wasn't such a chicken shit.

I hadn't always felt this way about Chloe. She'd joined Desert Vistas Construction just over three years ago as her second job out of college. For a while she'd worked as the assistant to the head of construction, but when my admin retired, she interviewed for the job. I'd hired her for her skills and her calm but focused personality. I'm embarrassed to say I hadn't really noticed her yet aside from her job performance.

It happened gradually, and at the same time, all at once. I'm a guy, so I knew that she was pretty. But oddly, I noticed her body last. Mostly because she dresses like she thinks she's ninety. Or she hates her body. She always looks neat and presentable, but her clothes aren't designed to get you to notice them, so I didn't.

What I did notice was her personality. How sweet she is, always remembering who's sick or who's having a birthday. She figured out that I skip a lot of meals when I'm on the go and then end up eating crap. Suddenly I was finding home-made granola bars in my briefcase, or a plate of pot roast she'd brought from home would appear on my desk in the middle of a conference call. She was always there. Always thinking of me. Not just taking care of my business, but taking care of me.

I was a little on guard at first, but she wasn't playing an angle. It didn't take me long to learn that this was just who Chloe was. She took care of people. After a few months, we were eating lunch together every day. Ostensibly for the purpose of going over work, but most of the time we'd end up talking. In the past few years Chloe had become one of my best friends. I loved her quiet sense of humor. The way she'd tell tiny fibs about unimportant things like what she thought of Alice in accounting, or if she was on another diet. Then she'd look to the side with such obvious guilt over her white lie I couldn't help but call her out.

That was the gradual part, the way she went from being my assistant to my partner in everything. My girlfriends gave me shit about not being able to commit, but why would I want to? I spent all day with Chloe, who was pretty much the perfect woman. The only reason I even bothered with other women was for sex. Honestly, I hadn't thought it all through that clearly. I was just living my life and enjoying myself.

Then it happened. Chloe and I were on site for a meeting. We'd gone out to look into some problems with a plumbing contractor. It was something I'd normally handle on my own, but she was setting up an event at the clubhouse on site and she needed to check the kitchen. We'd been crossing the site, headed from one of the spec homes, when a sudden spring rain shower had hit. Both of us took off for cover, but the water came down in sheets and we were soaked to the skin before we got to the clubhouse.

I'll never forget what happened to Chloe's boxy yellow shirt-dress under all that rain. Her hair was plastered to her face, and she was trying to pin it back up, but all I could see was her body. Holy Jesus, where the fuck had she been hiding that body?

Soaking wet yellow cotton was plastered to every inch of the curviest, most luscious shape I'd ever seen. Her tits alone were worth a portrait. Lush, round, and full, they almost overflowed what was probably a plain, serviceable bra. Her waist curved in, not tiny, but an hourglass compared to the flare of her hips. And her thighs, full but firm, her calves a smooth handful tapering down to her ankles.

My cock had hit full throttle after one look and it refused to go down. I had to drive back to the office with my jacket in my lap and made some excuse to get out of there for the rest of the day. My brain felt like it was going to explode.

Chloe was a goddess. A fucking goddess. I spent the rest of the day and the night planning how I was going to seduce her. Then I walked in the next morning to see her in another of her dull, boxy suits, all trace of that magnificent body gone, and realized that if I touched her I risked losing the best thing that had ever happened to me.

I'm not usually a pussy with women. To the contrary, getting a woman's attention has always been easy for me. I'm good looking, charming most of the time, and usually not an asshole. It doesn't hurt that I own my own company and do well financially. I'd had an active social life since I was fifteen and the neighbor's daughter decided to take me under her sexual wing during her summer off from college. Since then, I'd had no problems getting any woman I wanted. And thanks to that same neighbor's daughter, I knew what to do with them once I had them.

But Chloe was something else entirely. She wasn't some random lay. I couldn't fuck her and then forget to call her. She'd become more than just a friend. She was my touchstone. The one thing in my life that I could always depend on. She knew me inside and out. When she heard me start to get annoyed in a meeting she could just look up from her notebook and slant me a look, or send me a wink, and I'd calm down. I had no idea what I'd do without her. And no clue if she was even interested.

She'd never given me the slightest hint she might think of me as more than her boss and her friend. After the incident with the wet yellow dress, I'd watched her carefully, trying to read more into every move and gesture. But she was always proper, always correct. I got nothing more than the same easy affection combined with professionalism that Chloe had always given me.

In the end, I'd decided it wasn't worth the risk. If I came on to her, or made her uncomfortable, she might leave. Then what would I do? I thought about telling her how I felt, but I wasn't even sure what to say. I want you? You're my best friend? It all sounded so inadequate. Was it love? Was that what I'd been dancing around? Who the fuck knew? I kept my mouth shut and tried to pretend I had no idea what she looked like under those unattractive clothes.

For six months I'd been playing this game with myself. Pretending I didn't want Chloe while secretly spinning dreams of being with her in the back of my mind. I didn't do it on purpose. But I'd find myself thinking about her in random moments. Wondering what she'd think of the sofa I was buying, or if she'd want a pasta maker in the kitchen. Now I was at a crossroads. I had to make a decision one way or another.

I was going to help Chloe find her brother, there was no question about that. Then I was going to take the little shit aside and tell him to man up and stop hiding behind his sister every time he got his dumb-ass in trouble. In my opinion, her brother and her father were a good part of the reason I had to be so careful with Chloe.

Nolan leaned on her for everything and, as far as I could tell, their father pretty much checked out after their mother left them when they were little. So the men she'd grown up with were either users or they walked away. She didn't have a lot of history that taught her she could trust a man with her heart. And my track record wasn't that great, either. I had no problem getting women, but I'd never bothered to keep one. Not for long, anyway.

Now things had changed. She was going to be living with me until we dealt with Nolan. I had a real shot to get to her after work. To make her see me as a man, not a player with a different girl each week, but as the man I was inside. And I wasn't going to let her go. We were too close for me to believe she couldn't want me. I'd just have to show her how it could be with us before she got a chance to get scared. It was high time I stopped being such a wuss and made a move.

I looked over at her again, not liking the shadows under her eyes. While I thought he was an ass, I knew she loved Nolan. She must be terrified. I reached over to take her hand.

"We're going to find him, Clo. I promise."

Chloe gave me a wan smile and said, "I hope so."

CHAPTER FOUR
Chloe

Sam held my hand all the way back to his house. He wasn't usually so touchy, but I needed the anchoring warmth and I was grateful for it. The more I thought about Nolan, the more worried I got. What could he have done to have those men looking for him?

We pulled into the drive at Sam's house, a sleek, modern home he'd built himself based on the design of a renowned architect. Desert Vistas had built the whole community, but in my opinion Sam's house was the best. It sprawled out across the desert looking more like a sculpture than a home, all sleek lines and contrasting textures. Before I saw it I would have said that modern architecture wasn't my thing. In general it still isn't. Sam's house managed to be both art and a home at the same time. Still, it was huge, over eight thousand square feet, and in comparison to my small apartment it could be a little overwhelming.

He parked the truck in the four car garage and came around to help me down from my side. He always did that when we rode in his truck. It was jacked up with huge tires. Perfect for construction sites, terrible for a short woman. Usually he gave me his hand. This time he leaned in and lifted me out of the truck, sliding one arm behind my back and the other beneath my knees. I was so surprised I didn't even ask him to put me down.

When he didn't, but started into the house instead, I finally got my head in gear.

"Sam, what are you doing? I can walk," I said, squirming to get to my feet. His arms tightened, keeping me where I was.

"No," he said. "You scared the hell out of me tonight. I'm keeping you right here until I feel like putting you down."

I didn't know what to say to that. Sam walked at a sideways angle to ease us down the long hallway from the garage to the kitchen. I was just wondering how to handle this when we entered the kitchen and came face to face with Daniel, Sam's Dad.

I knew Daniel well. He was a construction foreman with Desert Vistas and he was in and out of Sam's office all the time. A gruff but kind man, he looked like an older version of Sam, except with dark hair. I'd always thought he liked me well enough, but he'd never seen me being carried into the house he shared with his son. Awkward.

"Hi Daniel," I said with a little wave. Looking up at Sam I said, "Will you put me down now?" He dropped his head and met my eyes.

"No. You're exhausted, just relax."

"Are you finally getting your ass in gear, kid?" Daniel inexplicably asked. I felt Sam shrug.

"Working on it. Chloe's having some problems. Her brother is missing, and some men broke into her place tonight. They said something about taking her if they couldn't find Nolan."

Daniel swore under his breath. I squirmed in Sam's arms again. "Put me down," I said, "so I can make some tea or something. Daniel, do you want a snack?"

Sam set me on my feet. "The tea you like is in the cabinet over the electric kettle. And I think some of those muffins you brought to work are in the pantry. We could probably all use some tea and something to eat."

Sam was being sweet. He hated the herbal tea I drank. Daniel liked it, which was why they had a box in the house. But Sam would prefer decaf. Glad to finally have something constructive to do, even if it was only making a light meal, I got busy in the kitchen. I loved Sam's kitchen.

It was spacious, with tall windows looking out over the swimming pool grotto on the lower level behind the house and out into the light of the city beyond. Long counters, tons of cabinet space and an oversized island perfect for a quick meal made it homey when it could have been too cold. Not to mention the state-of-the-art appliances. I'd drooled over the Viking range. Since I'd be staying here for a few days, I'd have to cook something in the kitchen just to get my hands on that Viking. I'd always wanted one of those.

I'd been here before a few times, mostly when we were having company parties. But making tea and toasting muffins felt oddly intimate. I got a mug of decaf going in the single cup brewer and listened to Sam fill his father in on the situation with Nolan. He hadn't gotten very far when I brought the drinks and toasted muffins to the table and took a seat. Daniel accepted his tea, pinned me with his Dad eyes and asked,

"So what's your plan to find your brother? Are you going to call the police about the break-in?"

I looked away. I should have called the police. I wanted to. Putting into words what I had barely admitted to myself, I said, "No. I can't. I'm afraid Nolan is in trouble and if I call the police I'll just make it worse."

"Then you need to call Axel," Daniel said with a slight nod. "Or let Sam do it."

"I'm not comfortable with that," I said, sipping my tea and looking away from both men.

"Chloe, you're not being reasonable," Sam said. "Axel can handle this. This is what he does. Explain to me why you won't call him."

"I know I should, but I have this feeling that if Axel gets involved this is all going to spin out of control."

"Honey," Sam said in a gentle tone I'd never heard before. "It's already out of control. Nolan is missing. From your description, the men in your place were armed. They're after you, not just Nolan. You're in danger."

"I want to handle this on my own," I said, my voice small.

I always handled Nolan on my own. I'd been solving his problems since he was in grade school and getting sent home for fighting and cheating on his homework. Our mom had walked out on us when Nolan was three and I was six. Our father had never been that interested in his children when our mother had been around. Once she left, he mostly forgot about us, lost in his own anger over her desertion and happy to leave us with a succession of babysitters. I'd been looking out for Nolan for so long, the idea of handing his problems over to someone else was terrifying.

As if he could read my mind, Sam took my hand and tugged, prompting me to look up and meet his clear blue eyes. They were kind and patient, all his earlier anger drained away. He watched me, seeing my panic and fear.

"Chloe, trust me, okay? Let me call Axel in and we'll let him help us."

"I still want to look for Nolan on my own," I said. I knew he was right. I needed help. But I wasn't willing to hand my problems to Axel and walk away. "We'll call Axel. But I'm not sitting here and letting him take over while I go on like nothing's wrong. I can't do that."

"Fine," Sam said. "But you have to promise me one thing. You stick with me. You don't go anywhere without me until we find out what's going on. Can you do that?"

"But we have work. You have meetings this week-"

"We'll reschedule what we can and work around the rest," Sam said, rubbing the back of my hand with his thumb. "We'll keep at it until we find Nolan. Okay?"

"Okay," I said doubtfully.

We had a lot going on in the office that week. We always had a lot going on. Sam and I couldn't both disappear at the same time. But I'd worry about that later. Taking a bite of the blueberry muffin in front of me, I looked up to see Daniel watching Sam's hand around mine. Suddenly self conscious, I tried to pull away, only to feel Sam tighten his grip. Not wanting to struggle with him in front of Daniel, I gave up and left my hand in his. To be honest, I liked it there. I liked it way too much.

Maybe he sensed that I was at my limit, because Sam changed the subject to the development project

Daniel was currently supervising and I zoned out. My worry for Nolan was exhausting, but under it was a new awareness that Sam was being weird. He called me 'honey' occasionally, but not often at all. Only a few times that I could remember. And he never held my hand. Why was he doing it now - in front of Daniel no less? It was odd. Maybe he was just trying to calm me down.

Except he hadn't let go when I'd pulled away. Or put me down when I'd asked him to. That wasn't like Sam. He could be forceful. And he liked to get his way. But he was generally pretty easy going unless he dug his heels in over something. It didn't make sense.

I finished my muffin and stood, taking our mugs and plates to the sink. Daniel and Sam stood as well. It was late, well past my usual bed time and I was tired. Daniel said goodnight to both of us and headed out of the kitchen, down the hall to the garage before taking a set of stairs to the lower level and his suite of rooms on the opposite side of the house from Sam's wing.

When Sam had built the house, he'd planned for Daniel to stay in the main level of the house and use those rooms for guests, but Daniel had had other ideas. Claiming he and Sam both needed their space, he'd taken the guest rooms as his own.

Which essentially left me alone with Sam. I couldn't tell you the last time I was uncomfortable around Sam, but with the way he was being weird and our arguments over Nolan, I felt a sense of unease, as if everything was off kilter. He stared at me in silence as if considering something. Or maybe I had muffin crumbs on my lip. I swiped the back of my hand across my mouth, but it came up clean. Sam's eyes narrowed.

"Time for bed," he said, reaching out to grab my hand once more. Still confused by his behavior, I let him. I wasn't expecting him to lead me down the hall I knew went to his bedroom.

"Where are we going?" I asked.

"Bed," he said shortly.

"But I thought the guest rooms were in the other wing."

"They are. But there's a pull-out in my office. I'm sleeping there. You'll be in my bed."

I stopped moving, forcing Sam to come to a halt or pull me over. "Sam, I'm not taking your bed. I'll just stay upstairs."

"No." He tugged on my hand again, but I refused to move. "I don't want you that far away," he said. "We have no idea who's after you or how far they'll go to get to you. I sleep like a rock. If something happened, and you were upstairs I'd never hear you. If you're in my room, they have to go right past me to get to you."

"But we're safe here. You have excellent security and the neighborhood is gated. Who could get to me?"

Sam crossed his arms over his chest and shook his head. "I'm not taking any chances with you, Chloe. You sleep in my room. I'm in the office. End of discussion."

I opened my mouth to protest and Sam lunged forward, shoved his shoulder into my stomach, and picked me up in a fireman's carry.

"Put me down," I shouted. "I'm too heavy, you'll hurt yourself."

In answer, he swatted my rear end. "You're not too heavy, for Christ's sake. I could carry you all day. Now shut up."

I didn't shut up. Ignoring my protests, Sam strode down the hall to his bedroom door. When we were inside, the door shut firmly behind us, I said,

"What are you doing? When did you turn into such a caveman?"

"When did you stop doing what I told you to?" he shot back. I couldn't help but laugh.

"I've never done what you told me to."

"True," he admitted. "But you're usually much more agreeable about it."

That was true. I'd never followed Sam's orders, not exactly. But I was generally fairly diplomatic when I disagreed with him. Part of that was him being my boss. But mostly it was just me. I could argue when I had to, but I was happier when everyone just got along. Maybe that's why I was so spun by everything that was happening. All this conflict was freaking me out.

Choosing not to fight with me anymore, Sam went to his dresser and came back with a dark grey t-shirt with 'Delecta' across the front in elaborate cursive. He handed it to me, saying,

"We'll deal with the rest of your stuff tomorrow, but you can sleep in this tonight."

I took the shirt and looked up at him. He'd stopped right in front of me, so close our shoes were almost touching, and stared down at me with a funny look in his eyes.

"What?" I asked, reaching up to touch my face again.

Why did he keep looking at me like that? In answer, he gave a shake of his head. Before I could step back, Sam reached out and wrapped his arms around me, pulling me tight into his chest. I stiffened in surprise, then relaxed into him. The scent of spice and citrus surrounded me as I rested my head against Sam's hard chest, soaking in his strength.

He drew back after a minute, his arms still holding me close. I tipped my head up to look at him and wasn't surprised to see that odd look back in his eyes. He lifted one hand to my face and curved his fingers under my chin, tilting my face to his.

"Chloe," he whispered. "I should have done this a long time ago."

Then, to my complete and utter shock, Sam Logan dropped his lips to mine. The kiss started slowly, mostly because I couldn't quite catch up. When his arm tightened around my back and his lips opened mine, I gasped at the heat of his tongue. I should have pulled away, but a kiss from Sam was every secret day dream I'd had since I'd first started working for him. I had no idea why he was kissing me, but this might be my only chance. Maybe Sam was just worried about me. Whatever it was, I wasn't going to let his kiss pass me by.

Pressing into him, I reached up and sank my fingers into his thick, soft hair, pulling his face into mine. I didn't have a ton of experience with kissing, but it didn't seem to matter. I moved my mouth against his, my tongue stroking his, our lips rubbing together, heat spiraling through my body.

Sam groaned deep in his chest and began to move, backing me into the wall without breaking the kiss. I kept my grip on his hair, loving the feeling of his head in my hands as his mouth fed from mine in kiss after drugging kiss. His hands were everywhere, stroking my back, my sides, untucking my blouse and sliding beneath to brand my bare skin with trails of heat. When his palm rose to graze the side of my breast, I whimpered.

Like a shot, he was gone, stepping back, dropping his hands and shoving them in the back pockets of his jeans.

"Sleep well," he said as if he hadn't just been holding me to the wall kissing the life out of me. "If you need anything, I'm right across the hall."

With that, he left. I stood there, leaning against the wall for a long minute before going to the bathroom to change into his t-shirt. I got into his bed, surrounded by his scent and tried to fall asleep, my head spinning from his kiss. What had that been about?

I'd never had any idea Sam might want to kiss me. I'd dreamed about it, but I hadn't imagined those dreams might ever come true. Not that they had, really. In my dreams he didn't kiss me breathless and then abruptly leave. What had he been thinking? Maybe he just hadn't been laid in a while, I was convenient, and then he thought better of it. But that wasn't like Sam. And anyway, I wasn't the kind of woman who stirred men to uncontrollable lust.

Had he kissed me as a distraction? So I'd stop thinking about Nolan? If he had, it hadn't worked. Now I had two things to worry about. My head pingponged between unsolvable problems, and I tossed and turned for hours before I finally managed to drop off into a restless sleep.

CHAPTER FIVE
Sam

What the fuck was that? I left Chloe alone in my room as calmly as I could, then strode across the hall to my office. Thank God I kept a decanter of whiskey in here even though I rarely opened it. Filling one of the crystal glasses with a good three fingers of liquor, I threw myself onto the leather couch and tossed the alcohol back, relishing the burn in my throat as I swallowed.

What the fuck had I been thinking? The idea was to seduce her. Slowly. Subtly. To make her see me as more than just her boss and her friend. If I could come to her rescue and be her knight in shining armor while we looked for her brother, that had to help my cause. Attacking her in my bedroom, shoving her against the wall, and kissing her until she couldn't breathe was not part of the plan.

But fuck, that kiss. She'd frozen at first, holding back as I'd pulled her closer. Once she'd gotten into it, she'd been like fire in my arms. Making little whimpers in the back of her throat, burying her fingers in my hair and pulling my face to hers. She'd wanted me to kiss her. If I'd stopped there, it might have been okay.

Instead I'd had to back her into the wall and get my hands all over her. Chloe was just too much temptation. That soft body and even softer skin. Her heat, her mouth, it was all too much, and I lost my head. The feeling of my palm stroking the side of her breast was almost enough to make me come in my jeans.

How sad was I? Totally out of control from one kiss. I'd been imagining kissing Chloe for months. To finally be doing it, my hands on her bare skin, the weight of her breast teasing my palm. Just thinking about it was killing me.

I tossed back the rest of the whiskey and got up. Acting before I could think better of it, I locked the door to my office and crossed the room, unzipping my jeans as I went. My cock was a steel bar, had been since well before I'd laid a finger on Chloe. I wanted to strip naked, go back into my bedroom and slide between the covers with her. Peel off the t-shirt I'd given her to wear and feast on her body.

I'd start between her legs, kiss her pussy like I'd kissed her mouth. After I made her come, I'd move up and spend some time on her breasts. A week might be long enough. And after that, when I'd had my fill of her breasts, I'd fuck her. Right then I thought I could fuck Chloe forever.

In reality, if I was really in bed with her, I'd probably last about a minute, I was so turned on. But that reality wasn't going to happen. At least not tonight. I couldn't afford to be distracted for long, so I stepped into the three quarter bath attached to my office and turned the shower on cold. Maybe between the icy water and my hand on my cock I could get my head back in the game.

With the sound of Chloe's whimpers in my ears and the memory of her breast in my hand, I gripped my cock and began to stroke, the slick soap against my skin giving me just the right friction. Not as good as her pussy would be, but it was enough for now. Pressing my forehead to the cool tile of the shower, I pictured Chloe's dazed eyes after our kiss, her ragged breathing, and the way her round, full breasts had looked the day we'd been caught in the rain.

The images swirled together into a dream Chloe, half naked, wet from the shower and eager for me. My eyes squeezed shut, I saw her as she dropped to her knees and took my cock in her mouth, soothing my need with hard, quick sucks. I wasn't sure if the real Chloe had ever had a dick in her mouth, but my dream Chloe sucked me like she wasn't afraid of my size. She took me deep and swallowed, letting the head of my cock into her throat. At the thought of how she'd look on her knees, her hungry eyes meeting mine, I came, my knees going weak as my orgasm painted the wall and was washed away.

I'd been stroking my cock to images of Chloe for months. But never after I'd just had her in my arms. If I didn't fuck this up, maybe the next time I'd get the real thing. I finished my shower, pulled my boxers back on, and unlocked my door, leaving it open so I could hear if Chloe needed anything.

Then I pulled out the sofa bed and put on the sheets. When I was finally ready for sleep I did two last things. First, I called Axel and filled him in. He promised to get to work on finding Nolan immediately.

After I hung up, I left a message for Lola, my personal shopper. Like a lot of guys with busy jobs, I had a need for a professional wardrobe and no desire to shop. At the suggestion of my friend Dylan, I'd tried outsourcing my shopping to Lola at Neiman Marcus. She was a miracle. And she'd recently outfitted Dylan's girlfriend with a whole new wardrobe.

Like Chloe, Dylan's girl had curves. And Lola had known exactly how to dress them up. Chloe needed her. I didn't care about the cost; I wanted Chloe to have whatever she needed. This was step two in my courtship.

I planned to use the excuse that she didn't have anything at my house to wear. I left Lola a detailed description of Chloe, including her sizes, which I'd taken from the tag on her suit jacket and the shoes she'd abandoned in the kitchen. Sometime tomorrow I'd get a real start on my pursuit of Chloe. And maybe she'd forget all about tonight's fuck-up. I could only hope.

CHAPTER SIX
Chloe

When I finally fell asleep, I tossed and turned, haunted by vague dreams in which Nolan came home, beaten and scared, and then Sam showed up to take me away before I could find out what was wrong. I didn't really pass out until just before dawn, then didn't wake up for hours. Usually I was up with the sun whether I wanted to be or not. Normally, my body sensed day break and switched itself on, even if I'd just gotten to bed.

Sam's room had heavy curtains along the wide, tall window. Very heavy curtains. They must have tricked my brain into thinking it was still night, because I slept until eleven. Sleep fell away slowly, and I rolled over in bed trying to get my bearings for a few minutes before I noticed the time. Realizing it was almost lunch, I bolted out of the bed and into the bathroom.

The heat of the shower soaked into me, calming

me down as I rummaged through Sam's shower for what I'd need. I'd found an unopened razor blade in a drawer, along with an unopened toothbrush. But I'd have to make do with his shampoo and other bath stuff. Squirting the shampoo into my palm I realized I had the source of the citrus side of Sam's scent. Looking closer at the bottle I saw it was a combination shampoo/conditioner/body wash. I smiled and shook my head as I massaged in the lather.

Sam was rolling in money and he couldn't be bothered to buy a separate shampoo and body wash. He'd grown his company into a huge success over the past ten years. By the time I'd joined Desert Vistas, they were already handling large scale developments in both Nevada and California. But Sam was still the same down-to-earth guy he'd always been.

Daniel had told me once that it didn't seem to matter if he was in a tract home or his ten million dollar architectural marvel, a tux or his jeans. He was still Sam. He might have been able to afford the most expensive soap on earth, but he still bought the normal stuff everyone else got at the grocery store.

I dried off and tried not to enjoy smelling like Sam. I hoped he'd be back to normal today. We had a lot of things to do. Meeting with Axel, probably. We had to go back to my place to see if anything had been destroyed. And I wanted to look for the number of one of Nolan's work friends to see if he knew anything. At some point we'd have to go in to the office.

He had contracts to review and I didn't even want to think about his inbox. Or mine.

Teeth brushed and hair combed, I looked around for my suit and blouse only to find them missing. I'd taken everything off the night before and laid them over the arm chair across from the bed. Now it was empty. Not sure what to do, I looked through Sam's huge closet and found a robe hanging on the back of the door. It was huge, dragging on the floor behind my heels, but at least it covered me.

Resigned to the fact that I wasn't going to find anything better, I tied it tight and went looking for Sam. His office door hung open, the pull-out still unfolded, the sheets half pulled up, as if he'd thought about making the bed and then changed his mind. I found him sitting on a stool at the bar in the kitchen, working on his laptop and sipping a cup of coffee. Seeing me hovering at the end of the hallway, he smiled.

"Finally awake?" he asked. "I thought you never slept in."

"I don't," I said, tucking my wet hair behind my ear. Without my hair pins, which had disappeared along with my suit, my hair was springing into curls and waves as it dried. I liked to keep it contained, thinking it more professional, but little strands were always falling out, no matter what I did.

"Are you hungry? Marte made you breakfast. It's in the warming oven. I ate a while ago."

He was smirking at me for sleeping in, but I ignored him. It seemed like he was back to normal. Good. As wonderful as that kiss had been, I couldn't afford for it to happen again. He was my boss, and I didn't want to leave my job. I found a plate of french toast stuffed with cream cheese and a bowl of sliced fruit. Yum.

I shouldn't eat it, but I was going to anyway. I'd been dieting lately - it felt like I was always dieting - but I was a stress eater, and with Nolan missing it didn't seem like that big a deal to eat the French toast. I was making myself a cup of coffee when I asked,

"Did she take my clothes to wash? I can't find my suit. Or my hairpins."

"No. I threw them out."

"What?" I almost spilled the full coffee cup in my hand when I whirled to face him. Sam was still studying his laptop screen and hadn't bothered to look up.

"What do you mean you threw out my clothes? You can't throw away my clothes. I need them."

"No you don't. Pick something off the table in the dining room."

I put my mug down on the kitchen counter and stormed past the bar and into the dining room. Like the model home I'd been hiding in the night before, Sam's house was an open plan on the main level. The great room, with its panoramic views of the Las Vegas strip, flowed into the kitchen on one side and the dining room on the other. I strode through, without admiring the view of desert and city, to find the long table completely covered in clothes. One end was stacked with shoe boxes and a chair was pulled out and covered in scarves and purses.

"WHAT IS THIS?!" I screeched. I'm not usually a screecher. Really. Not even a yeller. The stress of the past few days had me a little more emotional than usual, but I'm generally a pretty calm, level headed woman. This was just too much. I didn't even know what it meant. "Where did all of this come from?"

"I asked Lola to drop it by. It's for you," Sam said from right behind me. I jumped, glad I'd left my coffee in the kitchen or I would have spilled it all over me. He could move quietly when he wanted to.

"Why, Sam? I have clothes."

"Now you have new ones. Pick something to wear and I'll explain."

I surveyed the table, realizing on closer inspection that the clothes had been laid out as outfits, with accessories and shoes nearby. It was a dizzying array. I knew who Lola was, had even met her a few times when I needed to pick up a suit for Sam. She was elegant, with impeccable taste. I could see her hand in the wardrobe laid out on the table.

Suits, a few dresses, and embarrassingly, a pile of silk, satin, and lace that could only be lingerie. Even some loungewear, more elegant versions of the yoga pants and old t-shirts I usually wore after work.

Confused and not sure what to say to Sam, I picked up the closest suit, a light-weight raspberry wool with a coordinating cream shell sweater and silky scarf. Grabbing the matching slingback heels, underwear, and a bra, I turned and marched back to his bedroom without another word, hoping silence might accomplish what my screeching had not. Of course, since I wasn't exactly sure what was going on, I didn't really know what I was trying to do with my frosty quiet.

Maybe just get a little space to figure out what Sam was up to. Back in his room, I shut the door behind me and flipped the lock. Normally I'd never feel the need to lock the door against Sam, but nothing had been normal since Nolan had disappeared.

Stripping off the robe, I looked at the shell pink panties and bra in my hands and felt my cheeks turn red. Sam had purchased underwear for me. Not the plain cotton underwear and bras I got on sale at one of the big box stores. But real lingerie, the fabric was soft. The straps, wide enough to support my breasts, were both padded and embroidered so the bra was not only functional, it was beautiful as well. I didn't want to guess at what it must have cost.

My hands shaking a little, I threaded my arms through the straps and pulled the bra into place. Miraculously, it fit. How had he known my bra size? It was ridiculous to blush this hard when no one could see me, but the idea that he'd correctly guessed the size of my breasts and bought me underwear led my thoughts in directions I wasn't ready to explore.

Trying to stay focused, I pulled on the matching panties and contemplated the rest of my outfit. The suit was beautifully tailored, but I had my doubts about the skirt. In a pencil style, it was made to fit the hips, then flare out in kick-pleats just below the knees. Gorgeous. But my hips and pencil skirts were not friends. Never had been. Still, I couldn't wear the robe all day.

Resigned to a fight with the zipper and not being able to sit comfortably all day, I stepped into the skirt and pulled it up, putting on the sleepless cream shell on top first so I wouldn't be half naked while I fought with the skirt. To my shock, the skirt's zipper slid up with ease, the fabric conforming to my butt and hips perfectly, not a straining seam anywhere. Not ready to look yet, I slid my feet into the heels and my arms into the jacket. Holding the scarf in my hand, I turned to look in the floor length mirror on Sam's closet door.

I never would have picked a suit like this for myself. The color was too bright and the cut of the skirt would have scared me away. But the slightly dusky, rich raspberry pink wool suited the warm tones of my skin and light brown hair. And the fitted lines of the suit brought out the curves I was always trying to hide, making me look professional but still feminine.

I usually wore my hair in a bun, but without my pins it would have to stay down. The softer style looked good with the new suit. Torn between being annoyed at Sam and loving the outfit Lola had put together, I arranged the coordinating scarf and left the room, thinking that I needed the coffee I'd never had the chance to drink.

Striding into the kitchen, trying not to enjoy the feel of the new heels as they clicked against the hardwood floors, I froze when I saw Sam's face. Warned of my arrival by the sound of my shoes coming down the hall, he'd looked up to see me enter. His blue eyes widened and his mouth dropped just a little. Then, alarmingly, those intent eyes narrowed, and he scanned me from head to toe, his expression satisfied and proprietary.

I pretended to ignore the shiver that went down my spine at his look and headed for my abandoned coffee sitting on the counter. Sam got to it first. Standing to block me, he scooped up the coffee mug and poured it out into the sink.

"It's cold. Let me make you more." He set up the single-cup brewer and slid my mug into place, ready to be filled. Turning to face me, he gave me another once over. "You look beautiful," he said. "I'm throwing out the rest of your clothes, too. If everything Lola picked out looks as good as that suit, I'll have to lock you in the office to keep all the guys away."

I'm pretty sure my jaw dropped. Retorts spun in

my mind, so many I didn't know where to start. Sam had called me beautiful. He'd said I looked so good he'd have to lock me up. And he also said he was going to throw out the rest of my clothes. Clearly the visit to crazy town we'd taken last night when he'd kissed me was not over. My mind unable to process, I said the first thing that sprang to my lips.

"I don't understand."

"What don't you understand?" Sam asked, cocking an eyebrow at me. I'd always thought it was cute when he raised one eyebrow. At that moment I had the sudden urge to swat the arrogant expression off his face. I was unbalanced enough with Nolan missing. I didn't need Sam to go nuts on me at the same time.

"Everything. Why am I here? Why didn't you just take me to a hotel? And why would you ask Lola to buy me clothes? I have clothes." I didn't have the guts to mention the kiss the night before. Part of me still wondered if that had been a dream.

The coffee maker kicked on, and Sam concentrated on watching the cup fill with steaming liquid, avoiding my question.

"Sam?" I prompted in a quiet voice, beginning to worry. When the cup was full, he added a splash of cream, stirred and handed it to me. Leveling his eyes on my face, his expression serious, he said,

"I'm not sure you're ready to talk about this."

"I don't even know what this is," I answered,

drinking the hot coffee to cover my confusion.

"I know. I've handled everything with you the wrong way from the beginning. I can't fix that now. So we're starting from scratch. And if I fuck it up, you'll just have to bear with me."

"Sam," I said helplessly, his answer no answer at all. "What do you mean you handled me the wrong way?"

Leaning back against the counter, he picked up his own coffee and took a long sip, his eyes on my face. I couldn't tell if he was studying my expression or trying to think of what to say. Maybe both. Finally, he spoke.

CHAPTER SEVEN
Chloe

"Us," Sam said, still studying my face. "You and me. That's what I handled the wrong way. I thought I could have everything. You in the office and other women just to date. They never meant anything when I had you to come back to. But then I realized I didn't want anyone else. I only want you. And I'm done with wondering what to do about it. You're mine."

"What?" I asked, stupidly. I still wasn't getting it. Or I was afraid to get it, afraid of what it might mean. Or worse, that my hopes and dreams had caused me to completely misunderstand.

"You're mine, Chloe. You've been mine for three years and neither of us realized it. But I've finally figured out what to do with you. So you're staying here. And I bought you new clothes because you needed them. You deserve the best and I wanted you to have the best. So I got it for you. That's my job. To take care of you."

Speechless, I shook my head at him. "You're crazy," I said. "The only 'us' we can have is in the office. There can't be an 'us' outside of that."

"Why not?"

"Because I work for you," I said, frustration and confusion making my voice rise. "And I'm not the kind of woman who has an affair with her boss."

"I'm not talking about an affair," Sam said, his own voice rising.

"Then I don't get it. You want to go out with me?" I asked, hesitantly, terrified I'd misread him and he was going to start laughing.

"I think we're past that stage, don't you?" Sam said, laughing just a little. "I've spent more time with you than most men have with their wives."

"That was work."

"Was it only work? At lunch? Or the conversations we'd have in the car? Was that just work for you?"

I might have continued to argue with him, but the faint note of uncertainty in Sam's voice disarmed me. Instead, I shook my head.

"No, of course not," I said. "But we can't get involved. I'd have to quit."

"Who said anything about you quitting?" Sam asked, alarm spreading across his handsome features. "You can't quit."

"Well what would we do when you moved on?" I asked, trying to make him understand what it would be like from my perspective. He went from partner to partner, commitment never a big deal for him. I'd slept with one man in my life and I'd had only a few boyfriends since college, all short term. I wasn't built for a casual affair.

"Who said I was going to move on?" Sam asked.

At that, I rolled my eyes and took another sip of my coffee. I loved Sam. I had for a long time. But he wasn't made for long term monogamy any more than I was for sleeping around.

The impossibility of the whole thing somehow made me feel like I was back on solid ground. Putting my mug on the counter, I got my breakfast back out of the warming oven where Sam must have put it while I got dressed and sat on one of the stools tucked beneath the island. "Chloe," he said, interrupting me, "I'm serious."

Cutting my french toast into smaller squares, I resisted the urge to meet his eyes. "I know that you think you are, Sam. But this isn't a good idea. I can't have a relationship with you outside of work and still be your assistant. Maybe you could handle it, but I can't. And I won't sleep with you just because you've decided you want to have an affair with me."

"I'm not talking about an affair," he yelled, startling me. Taking a breath, he lowered his voice. "I'm not talking about an affair. I'm talking about a relationship. Between us." I was shaking my head before he could finish.

"No. It wouldn't work," I said, taking a bite of French toast to cover my uncertainty. My heart hurt and I felt a little nauseous. For the first time in my life, I had absolutely no interest in breakfast, even one created with the culinary talents of Sam's housekeeper. I was in love with Sam. I knew that. And I truly, deeply, sincerely did not want him to know that.

Sam was a good man. But he wasn't going to fall in love with me. He cared for me. I knew that he did. We had a great friendship. And I loved working for him. I had no idea why he suddenly wanted to change our relationship, but sleeping together would ruin everything.

He'd eventually grow tired of me as he did every woman he slept with. He'd move on and I'd be shattered. Destroyed. I had no illusions that my heart could survive sleeping with Sam intact. I'd fall even deeper in love with him and it would break me when he left.

"So that's it?" he asked, interrupting my thoughts.

"Yes. That's it. Let's just forget we had this conversation and go back to normal."

"And you'll forget I kissed you?"

At the memory of that kiss, I flushed and looked away. I'd never forget he'd kissed me. I was going to hold on to that kiss, remember it so often I'd never lose a single detail. This whole idea might be crazy and impossible, but I would always have that one perfect kiss from Sam.

"I can change your mind," Sam said, his eyes locked on my face with a predatory gleam. Meeting them, I drew in a deep breath, steadying myself for what I was going to say.

"I'm sure you could. You know exactly what you're doing with a woman, and I'm practically a virgin. You could probably seduce me in your sleep. I'm asking you not to try. Please just let this go, Sam."

He was silent for a long moment, still studying my face. His eyes had flared when I'd admitted my inexperience. That was probably a mistake. Sam could be easy going, but he was still an alpha male and admitting vulnerability was like waving a red flag in front of a bull. After what felt like a year, he said,

"You don't trust me."

"That's not it," I protested. "You're my closest friend, Sam. I do trust you. But this would be a bad idea. Give it some time and you'll see that I'm right."

"No. You don't trust me, Clo," he repeated. "You think I'm just interested in what I want and I'm not thinking about you. Like you're some new shiny toy or a momentary distraction that I'll get bored with and forget. As if I could ever get bored with you."

"Sam, don't do this."

"Fine, I won't," he said easily, his change of heart throwing me off balance. "We have bigger things to worry about. Nolan is missing. You're in danger. But

I'm not going to forget about this."

"Sam," I started to say. He cut me off.

"No. Shut up for a second and let me talk." Surprised, I did.

Sam wasn't always polite. He ran a construction company - some of the things I'd heard him say on the job could blister your ears raw. But he was always a gentleman with me. Or, he was most of the time. I couldn't recall him ever telling me to shut up before.

"I'll make a deal with you," he went on. "I'll back off for now. But you agree to stay with me until we resolve whatever is going on with Nolan. And you keep the clothes Lola brought over. Consider it a bonus from the company if that makes you feel better."

"Okay," I said, relieved. "And we can just forget we ever had this conversation?"

"No fucking way," Sam said. He sat down on the stool beside me and leaned his shoulder into mine, his mouth dropping beside my ear. Whispering, he said, "I know you're scared Chloe. I know you don't trust me and you're afraid I'm going to hurt you. But I'm not. I've wanted you for longer than you know and I'm tired of pretending I don't. If you can't believe what I say, I'll just have to show you how I feel."

He rose from the stool and left the kitchen, saying over his shoulder, "Finish your breakfast and we'll go check out your place. I'm going to get a few things together for the office."

Then he was gone, leaving me staring at my half

eaten French toast and wondering what the heck had just happened.

CHAPTER EIGHT
Chloe

My apartment was a mess. Cushions torn off the couch, food hanging out of the fridge, flour strewn on the floor. Our bedrooms, mine and Nolan's, were both equally destroyed. His might have been worse, but it hadn't been neat to start with, so it was hard to tell if the disarray was new or pre-existing.

For the first time since I'd seen the clothes on Sam's table, I wasn't conflicted about my new wardrobe. Everything in my closet had been torn from the hangers and thrown on the floor. The drawers were emptied. The things on my night stand had been swept to the carpet.

"I can't tell if they were looking for something or just really pissed off," Sam said, joining me in my bedroom.

"I know. I guess I should say thanks for the clothes now," I said, a quaver in my voice. Sam's arms came around me and I rested my head against his chest, grateful he was here with me. He'd been right, we had more important things to worry about right now than our stupid argument. Like what to do about the men who had trashed my apartment.

It was bad enough that they were after Nolan. But looking at the deliberately torn pair of underwear on the floor by my foot, I shivered. This wasn't just a search. This was rage. Whatever happened, I did not want these men to find me. Sam tightened his arms around me and gave me a squeeze.

"Let's get out of here, honey. Axel's guys can go through this stuff and see if there's anything to find. They know what they're doing. And I don't think it's safe here."

"Okay," I said, too shaken to argue. He was right. I'd thought if I came home to look around I'd spot a clue. But I wasn't Nancy Drew. All I saw was a mess. "Let me just get some stuff from my bathroom and then we can go to work."

The bathroom I shared with Nolan was largely untouched. A box of face powder I rarely used had been knocked to the floor, but most of my make-up and other toiletries were intact, if not where I'd left them. I packed my travel bag, sorting through the disarray to separate my things from Nolan's. Of the many things I didn't love about my brother moving in with me, sharing a bathroom was at the top of the list.

Almost done, I was leaning into the shower to grab my shampoo when I spotted a flash of lime green paper wedged half under the bottom of the toilet, as if it had fallen out of a pocket and been pushed aside by a careless foot. Picking it up, I saw it was a matchbook. A sketch of a pool table was on one side with the name 'Balls and Sticks'. Creative. On the other side someone, not Nolan, had written 'Feliks'. I froze.

I knew that name. The guy with the gun had said it the night before. Shoving the last of my stuff in a bag, I brought the matchbook out to Sam, who was looking through the books and DVD's that had been dumped out of my bookcase.

"I found this in the bathroom," I said, holding it out to him. "The guy with the gun last night said that name. Is that a pool hall? Do you think he's there?"

Sam turned the matchbook over in his hand, studying it. "Maybe. I'll give this to Axel."

"We should go check it out," I said. It was a lead. An actual lead that might get us to Nolan. We could give it to Axel, but I still wanted to follow it up.

"No. We should go to work. Axel can find this Feliks guy."

"Sam. We talked about this last night. We'll give everything to Axel, but I'm not sitting at home waiting for him to find Nolan. I can't do that. He has other clients, other responsibilities. I don't. I have Nolan."

"Honey," Sam said with a sigh, taking my arm and leading me to the door, "You need to let him grow up. Your whole life can't be about Nolan."

"It's not," I said, pulling my arm out of his grip and beating him out the door. I hated it when he gave me a hard time about my brother. Sam would never understand. I'd practically raised Nolan. He might be a mess, but he was mine.

"No?" Sam asked, his hand on my arm again in a tight grip as he walked me out of the building. "You can be pissed at me all you want, honey, but stay close. I don't like being here when we don't know what's going on."

I didn't answer, but relented, allowing him to tuck me into his side as we walked. He was right. It had been a risk to go back to the apartment, though I was glad we had. At least we knew a little more than we did before. Whoever those men were, they'd been looking for something, not just for me and Nolan. And we had a name and a location to start our search for Nolan. Feliks at Balls and Sticks.

I let Sam lead me to the truck and help me in, both annoyed and grateful for his protection. Once the doors were shut, and he'd started the drive to work, I said,

"I'm going to this place to find Feliks."

"No way," Sam said immediately.

"I'm not asking, Sam. I'm telling you what I'm going to do."

"And I'm telling you no fucking way."

Supremely aggravated by his bossy attitude, I said, "You're not my father, Sam. You don't get to tell me what to do."

"Well maybe if your father had bothered to say 'no' once in a while, we wouldn't be in this mess."

"Maybe we wouldn't," I said quietly. "But he didn't. He was a terrible dad, and he left raising Nolan to me. And I completely messed it up. I know that. But I'm going to fix it, Sam. I have to." Sam swore and pulled the truck into a parking lot as I whispered again, "I have to."

He threw the truck into park and turned to me, taking my face in his hands. "I shouldn't have said that, love, it was a shitty thing to throw at you. Your dad is an asshole, but that isn't your fault. And Nolan being a fuck up isn't your fault either."

"I raised him," I said quietly.

"And who raised you, Clo?" Sam asked in a gentle voice. I didn't answer. I didn't have to. We both knew the answer was that no one really had.

"You raised yourself," Sam went on, "And you're the most amazing woman I know. So you did something right. Whatever is going on with Nolan isn't on you. We'll find him because he's your brother and you love him. But don't blame yourself for this. He's twenty-two years old. He makes his own decisions. You're only three years older than him. Hardly old enough to baby-sit him, much less be responsible for him."

Sam waited for me to respond, but I didn't know what to say. He was right. When he put it like that it was absurd for me to feel more like Nolan's mother than his sister. I'd been barely more than a child when my Mom had left and our Dad stopped caring about us. Still, logic couldn't shake my sense of responsibility. Nolan would always be my little brother. To make Sam feel better, I said,

"I know."

"Okay," Sam said, dropping his hands from my face to place a kiss on my forehead.

"I'm still going to the pool hall," I said.

"Fine," Sam said, the gentleness burned out of his voice by his renewed anger. "But you're not going without me."

"Fine," I said. I hadn't planned on it, but I wasn't telling Sam that. For a laid back guy he'd been having some serious mood swings lately. I didn't tell Sam that either. Somehow I didn't think he'd take it well.

I was lost in thought as we pulled back onto the main road, trying to take in Sam's sweetness in sticking up for me against my own guilt and wondering what Axel would find out about Feliks. Out of the blue, I thought about Nolan's job. I'd called Monday morning and asked to talk to him, only to find that he'd been fired a few weeks before.

I'd been too worried about him to process that he'd lost his job. I could yell at him about that when I found him. But before the destruction in the apartment had distracted me, I'd meant to call one of his friends. He didn't hang out with a lot of the guys there, but he had been friends with a programmer named Tim. It was possible Tim knew something. Frantic to find out, I started digging around in my purse.

"What?" Sam asked, his eyes flicking off the road to watch me digging for my phone.

"I just thought of a friend of Nolan's I can call. From his job."

"Did you call them to let them know he was missing?" Sam asked. I hadn't mentioned the situation with Nolan's job yet. I hadn't wanted to hear what Sam would say.

"Not exactly," I admitted, dreading Sam's commentary when he found out Nolan had been fired. Again. "I called hoping he'd shown up, and they told me they let him go a few weeks ago."

"And he didn't tell you?" Sam asked, his voice flat. I shook my head. Sam took my hand in his.

"I'm sorry, honey."

That was it. No barbs about Nolan being irresponsible or needing to get it together. Just 'I'm sorry'. My heart squeezed in my chest. If I thought there was a chance I could get involved with Sam and have it work out, I'd be all over him. I couldn't bring myself to trust that he was serious about me, but he was such a good guy.

Finding my phone, I reluctantly withdrew my

hand from Sam's and started looking for Tim's number. I'd never called him, but a while ago Nolan had lost his phone and gave me Tim's number in case I needed to call when they were going out. I never erased my texts, so it had to be in here somewhere.

We were almost at work when I found it. I dialed and listened to the phone ring, a knot in my stomach.

"Hello? Nolan?" Tim's voice echoed through the speaker.

"No, it's Chloe, Tim. I'm looking for Nolan. Have you seen him?"

"No. I've been calling him. We were supposed to hang out the other night, but he didn't show. I thought maybe he lost his phone, and he was calling from yours."

"No. I wish. So you have no idea where he is?" I asked, the knot in my stomach getting worse. I don't know why I'd thought Tim would be able to help. At this point I was grasping at straws.

"To be honest, I'm kind of worried about him," Tim said. "He said some things when we last talked that made me think he was into some weird stuff."

"Like what?" I asked.

"Stuff I don't want to talk about on the phone," he said. "Can you meet me after work?"

"Sure. Just tell me where," I said, eager for any information he could give us.

"That coffee house down the street from where we work. Where Nolan used to work. You know-"

"I know where you mean, Tim. When? Five?"

"A little after. I'll see you then."

He hung up, and I did the same. As soon as I put the phone down, Sam said,

"So he knew something? We're meeting him after work?"

I told him what Tim had said and tried not to worry about what it might mean. Sam pulled the truck into the parking lot in front of the office and came around to help me out.

Despite my concern over Nolan, it was time to get in gear. We had a day's work to do, and between my sleeping late and stopping by my apartment, we were late. Really late. Sam held open the front door, a sheet of glass trimmed with polished wood and stone that opened into a high-ceilinged lobby with a slate floor and matching front desk. We both smiled and nodded at the receptionist who was speaking quietly into her headset.

The building had been designed by the same architect who created Sam's house. It was a testament to the quality of construction and design that Desert Vistas produced. Both elegant and desert rustic, it was a piece of art as much as an office building. Every time I passed through the door, it reminded me of Sam. As we walked to the executive suite, I ran over the day in my mind.

"You have a conference call on the Givvins project in forty-five minutes," I said, double checking the time on my phone. "The power point and the spreadsheets are in the file. I updated them with the latest numbers from John before I left last night."

Sam walked into his office and I followed, dumping my purse on my chair as I went on, "The preliminary contracts for the golf resort are on your desk. Jack marked anything he thought you should pay extra close attention to. Otherwise they're what you agreed to."

"What did you think?" Sam asked as he shrugged of his jacket. I tried not to be distracted by the way his button-down pulled across his broad shoulders. I didn't know why, but I'd always loved the way he looked when he took off his jacket. I yanked my mind back onto the contract.

"It was fair. But they tried to wiggle on the due diligence for the land. It's not what you agreed to."

"How much did they take off?"

"Seventeen days," I said. Sam whistled. We spent another few minutes going over business before I left the office and went to make us a pot of coffee. I usually drank the tea Sam hated in the afternoon, but today was a coffee day. A few minutes later I was sliding a steaming mug in front of Sam, along with a leftover muffin. I didn't know how much he'd eaten for breakfast, but he'd missed lunch, and he'd be hungry.

As I moved around his desk to get back to my own, he reached out to grab my hand, pulling me to a halt. "Thanks," he said, his eyes meeting mine with a heat that made me momentarily dizzy. "You look gorgeous in that suit. Don't let any of the guys hit on you while I'm busy."

He said it smiling, but gave my hand a squeeze before he let me go and I couldn't tell if he was joking. We did work with a lot of men, it was usually that way in a male dominated field like construction, but none of them ever hit on me. I was Sam's executive assistant. Not eye candy. And he'd never worried about the other men before.

Or maybe he had, and I just hadn't noticed. Shaking my head, I went back to my desk, determined to catch up on work and forget about everything else, just for a little while.

CHAPTER NINE
Chloe

It was one of those afternoons when the office was practically deserted, everyone either holed up working on projects or out in the field, so I was actually able to make headway into my pile of things to do by the time it was five o'clock. Sam walked out of his office door, briefcase in hand, just as I was preparing to go get him.

The afternoon had been completely normal, with no hint of the earlier tension between us. I might have wondered if I'd imagined it, except for his hand on my lower back as he walked me out through the lobby. He usually opened doors and helped me into his truck, but he rarely touched me more than he needed to.

I looked out of the corner of my eye to see if the receptionist noticed, but she was already gone for the day. The coffee house was a short trip, one we made mostly in silence. Sam seemed distracted, and I was preoccupied with wondering what Tim would have to tell me about Nolan.

We arrived at the coffee shop fifteen minutes after five to find Tim already there, waiting in the back, his fingers drumming nervously on the table. He was a skinny guy, with the sloppy clothes and negligent grooming stereotypical of most programmers, complete with pale skin and a geeky t-shirt. This one read 'Any fool can use a computer. Many do.'

Tim worked, and Nolan used to work, for a start-up that offered partially automated customer service bots for companies to cut down on actual people providing service. Instead of outsourcing the work to other countries, they were allowing the positions to be filled by bots. Nolan had seemed to like the job, but maybe he hadn't. It was turning out that I didn't know as much about my brother as I thought I did.

Tim's eyes widened when he saw me and he smiled in welcome. Then he noticed Sam behind me and scowled.

"Who is that?" he asked.

"My friend Sam," I said, sitting down across from Tim, "He's helping me look for Nolan. You really haven't seen him?"

"I don't know if I want to talk with him here," Tim said, reminding me of a sullen child.

"Why not?" I asked. "He's just a friend who's helping me."

Tim eyed Sam warily. "Fine," he said. "I don't know all that much."

He shifted in his chair, rubbing his palms on his jeans, his eyes flicking between Sam and me, beads of perspiration on his forehead. I'd only met Tim a few times, but I didn't remember him being this edgy. I was glad Sam was with me. Leaning in close so I could lower my voice, I said,

"Tim, please just tell me what you know about Nolan. I won't get you into trouble, I promise. Neither will Sam."

"Hey, I didn't do anything wrong," Tim said, shaking his head. "But Nolan got mixed up with some bad guys. He was playing cards a lot at night and he started playing in a room I heard belonged to Sergey Tsepov. Then he asked to borrow money from me."

"Did you give it to him?" I asked. Tim shook his head, shuffling his feet under his chair and wiping his palms on his jeans again.

"I didn't have it. And I know how it goes in this town. Never lend money to a guy who likes cards."

"Where is the room he's been playing?" I asked. Sam took my hand and tried to get my attention, but I ignored him, focused on Tim. If Nolan had been playing cards there a lot, maybe we'd get a better lead on where he was.

"315 Studen Street. You have to go in the back of the bar and talk to a guy named Dog to get in the game. I went with him once, but Dog freaked me out. He's the only one of those guys who wasn't Russian, and he looked like a biker."

"Okay." I stood when Sam grabbed my arm and practically dragged me to my feet. I tried to jerk my arm away, but he refused to let go, instead lacing his fingers with mine and pulling me in close. Before he could force me out of the coffee shop, I said to Tim, "Thanks, Tim. If you hear from Nolan, please, will you call me?"

He nodded, his eyes wide and kind of glazed as he watched Sam steer me through the chairs and tables and out the door. As soon as we were outside, I hissed, "What do you think you're doing?"

Sam opened the door to the truck and lifted me inside, his face dark, his eyes foreboding. He shut the door and rounded the front to get in, pulling his phone out as he went. He was already talking when he got in.

"… Yeah. Says he's been playing in one of Tsepov's rooms. On Studen. Fuck. I know. Call me when you know more. Thanks."

"Axel?" I asked, unnerved by how angry Sam seemed to be. He gave a short nod. "Are you going to tell me what has you so upset?"

"Has your friend in there always been a tweaker?" Sam asked. I had no idea what he was asking.

"I don't know what that means."

"He was high, honey. Based on the fidgeting,

dilated pupils, paranoia and sweating, I'm guessing meth."

"I don't know," I said, looking down at my lap. I didn't know anything about drugs. My dad was a drinker, and I'd always shied away from alcohol and drugs, afraid that whatever weakness drove my Dad to drink was hiding inside me as well. A horrifying thought occurred to me. "Do you think Nolan was doing drugs?"

"Did he act like Tim was? Paranoid, moving all the time, going without sleep?"

"No. Sometimes he came home really late, but then he'd pass out and I'd have a hard time getting him up for work. I guess he was out playing cards."

"Sounds like it. I doubt he was on drugs, but if he's tied up with Tsepov, then you're out of this, Chloe. All the way out."

"Why? We finally have something to go on, you can't tell me I'm out of it."

"Axel is going to the card room tonight. He'll talk to Dog. He knows him, he can find out more than you can."

"Then I'll go to the pool hall and talk to this Feliks guy."

"Chloe, just stay home and let Axel handle it," Sam said, clearly exasperated.

"No. I have to find Nolan. The sooner I find him, the sooner everything can go back to normal."

"You're being irrational."

"I'm not. You're trying to control my life," I said. "If you're just going to get in my way, then take me to a hotel and I'll do this on my own."

"No fucking way," Sam said. He pulled the truck in front of a pizza place we both knew and turned the engine off.

"Why are we here?" I asked, confused.

"Dinner," he answered, starting to get out. I put out a hand to stop him.

"Don't get pizza. Take me to the store and I'll get something I can cook."

"You don't have to cook Chloe."

"I know I don't. But I like to cook. It relaxes me. And you have an awesome kitchen."

Sam sat back and shut the car door. I was annoyed with him, but I still wanted to get my hands on his kitchen. Anyway, Daniel would be there and he wasn't annoying me. He shouldn't get stuck with pizza because his son was an ass.

Crossing my arms over my chest as we drove to the grocery store, I said, "I'm going to the pool hall tonight. You don't have to come if you don't want to." I had my car. At some point that morning, it had appeared in the driveway of Sam's house. I'd noticed it when we left for work.

"You need to stay out of this, Chloe."

"He's my brother."

"And Tsepov is Russian mob. I do not want you

on this guy's radar. It's bad enough if your brother is mixed up with him."

"If he's so bad, how do you know him?" I asked. Sam didn't exactly spend a lot of time hanging out with criminals. To my surprise, he looked out the side window, avoiding my eyes.

"He's got an interest in concrete."

"YOU'VE WORKED WITH HIM?!" I shouted. There I was, yelling for the second time in one day. But it wasn't often I found out my boss and best friend was doing business with the mob.

"Not the way you're thinking. Not once I knew who he was. Axel filled me in and I've kept an eye out where my business interests cross with Tsepov's. He's a smart man, but he's dangerous. You need to stay away from him."

"Fine, then Axel can go to the card room. But I'm still going to find this Feliks guy at the pool hall."

Sam sighed again. "I'll ask Axel. If the pool hall is Tsepov's, we're not going. If it's clean, I'll take you after dinner."

"Fine," I said, aware that to disagree would be unreasonable. I wanted to find Nolan. I did not want to get mixed up with the Russian mob.

We pulled into the grocery store closest to Sam's house and I pushed my problems out of my mind for a while. There was nothing I could do in the next few hours except try to relax by cooking a nice dinner in

Sam's amazing kitchen. So that's what I was going to do.

Mentally rifling through recipes, I almost didn't notice when Sam slid his arm around my shoulders as we entered the store. I thought about shrugging him off, but I couldn't bring myself to do it. However wrong my brain said it was to take a risk on Sam, something deep inside me thought it was very, very right.

CHAPTER TEN
Sam

So far the day had been a frustrating combination of one step forward and two steps back. Chloe was keeping the clothes I'd bought her, and she'd agreed to stay in my house, but she'd shut down my overtures so completely at first I'd worried that she had no interest in ever letting me break through.

I wasn't going to accept that. Not after the way she'd kissed me the night before. Chloe never would have kissed me with so much passion if she didn't want me. I knew she cared for me. I just had to find a way to get her to trust me. If she wouldn't accept that I was serious about her, I'd maneuver around her. At least that was my plan. It had been working so far.

I went in for a kiss, she'd push me away. So I stuck with the little things. Small touches. My arm around her. I'd figured out that she liked my easy affection, even leaned into me for more, as long as it wasn't too overt. I was going to prove to her that she was mine. No matter how long it took.

We got home from the grocery store, and Chloe went to change, trading that sweet pink suit for a pair of stretchy dark green pants that hung loose around her legs but hugged her curvy ass so well I had to fight not to touch her. With it she wore a matching hoodie and tank top. It was comfy and fine for wearing around my Dad, but still undeniably sexy.

She was in the kitchen seasoning the chicken when Dad got home. At the sight of her cooking, he raised his eyebrows at me and gave me a look. He'd liked her for me from the start, but I'd always told him I wasn't interested. I don't know how he does it, but the second my feelings for her changed, he knew. He'd been on my ass ever since. I was doing this my way. As much as Dad liked Chloe, he didn't know her like I did.

What came after was one of the best dinners we'd had in a long time. I had a professional grade kitchen, but neither of us cooked. We ate a lot of takeout, more than half the time sitting on the couch watching a game. With Chloe there, we ate at the table which Marte had cleared of her things while we were gone.

I'd been very pleased to find that Marte had made space in my closet for Chloe's new wardrobe. More clothes had arrived while we were gone. Chloe hadn't said anything, and I wondered if she'd noticed.

I was almost there. I had Chloe living in my house, her clothes in my closet, and she was sleeping in my bed. I just needed to join her there, and my life would be perfect. But we weren't that far yet. And I had a feeling the conversation that took place after dinner had set me back. Again.

My guard was down when she left to change for the pool hall. I was full of the roasted chicken, veggies, and garlic mashed potatoes. The woman could seriously cook. It wasn't why I wanted her. I'd eat takeout happily if I could eat it with Chloe. But her skills in the kitchen were a definite bonus. We'd tried to talk her out of the plan to find Feliks during dinner, but she'd dug in her heels. Dad and I were both a little mystified.

Chloe was smart. She was reasonable. Sensible. And reserved. Shy. Barreling into a pool hall was the last place she should want to go. She should have backed down and agreed to let Axel handle everything. It was the intelligent thing to do.

Instead she was insistent that she find Nolan herself. I understood that she loved her brother, but she was putting herself in danger she didn't understand. Maybe she was right, maybe I didn't get it. Because as far as I could see, Nolan wasn't worth all this trouble, brother or not. He'd never done anything but take from her. She deserved more. When we found him, I planned to make it clear that his days of freeloading off Chloe were over.

I was sitting at the table thinking about what I was going to do to Nolan when we caught up to him, when Chloe walked out into the kitchen dressed for the pool hall. I almost swallowed my tongue.

I'd never seen her dressed like that. She wore black spike heels with an open toe that displayed shiny red toenails. Tight jeans cupped her ass the way I wanted to and a dark red clinging top with a scoop neck that showed way too much cleavage. They were completely un-Chloe clothes.

"What are you wearing?" I asked, my voice strangling in my throat. She looked down at herself and then back up at me.

"What? I don't have much that's casual. Unless you think I should wear a cocktail dress? Or what I was wearing during dinner?"

"No. Of course not. But that's too-" I cut myself off and her face fell. She tugged on the top, pulling it out where it clung to her rounded waist. Shit. I should have known she'd think I was saying she looked fat. She was always worried about being overweight.

I didn't think she was overweight. I thought she was just the right weight. But the one time I'd told her that, she'd skewered me with a look and asked if I thought bigger women were beautiful, why did I date skinny models all the time?

I hadn't had a good answer. The truth was that I liked them too. I liked all different shapes on women, though too skinny had always been a turn off.

And the other truth is that I'd been lazy. The model types were the women who came on to me. They were there, they were beautiful, and they were easy. But neither of those truths made me look particularly good, so I'd kept my mouth shut, probably making it worse. Exactly like I was doing just then.

Dad came to my rescue and said, "You look gorgeous, Chloe. I think what has Sam's panties in a twist is that he doesn't want to take you to a scummy pool hall where you're going to attract attention from a bunch of men he normally wouldn't want anywhere near you."

She looked at me and I shrugged helplessly. "I know you're going to say I can't tell you what to do. But every man in that pool hall is going to be all over you, even with me there. Axel specifically said it wasn't the kind of place I'd want to take you."

"You already told me that," she said, shifting her weight as she opened her small purse and began to look through it. "I'm still going."

"I know." Unfortunately, Axel said that the place wasn't Tsepov's as I'd thought it would be and I'd lost the upper hand on insisting we give it a pass. "I wish I still had your other suit."

She looked up from her purse and met my eyes in confusion. "You said it was ugly."

"It was. I wish you could wear it tonight."

She shook her head at me as if I was a silly child and went back to looking through her purse.

"Clo," I said, "have you ever been to a pool hall before?"

"No," she answered absently. "We had a pool table at home when I was growing up so I always played there."

This time I shook my head at her. She had no idea what we were getting into. I'd never been to Balls and Sticks, but I recognized the neighborhood. This wouldn't be an upscale club with spotless felt on heavy wooden tables. This was going to be cracked neon signs and crappy bottled beer. I'd dressed down too, in the jeans and boots I wore on site, an old t-shirt, and my nine millimeter at my back. Thanks to Axel I'd gotten a license to carry concealed, and I'd never been happier about it.

Finally finished with whatever she was doing with her purse, she slid her ID and a small red tube into the front pocket of her jeans and looked up at me. "Are we going?"

"I guess we are," I said, positive I was going to regret it.

CHAPTER ELEVEN
Chloe

Sam drove us to the pool hall in silence, the whole time looking like he'd swallowed a toad. I didn't get what the big deal was. For one thing, I wasn't dressed to attract guys. I was wearing a knit top and jeans. Okay, the heels were sexy, and the top showed a little cleavage, but only a little. It was tasteful cleavage, not prowling-for-a-man cleavage. Same for the shoes. They were awesome, but I could have worn them to work with the right suit. Sam was either trying to flatter me, or he had a warped sense of what other men would find hot.

As we traveled through the streets of Vegas, we left the areas I knew and ventured into a darker side of town. Literally. Here every third streetlight was out, and more than a few of the stores were closed down. What had Nolan been doing on this side of the city? This was Vegas. If he'd wanted to play pool there were plenty of places closer to our apartment.

Finally, we pulled into a strip mall and parked in front of a building with a flickering neon sign over the door reading "Balls a d St cks". This must be it. I couldn't get an impression of what the place was like because the street facing windows had been covered with dark plastic from the inside. I was suddenly very glad I didn't have to open the door and go in by myself.

Sam did the job for me, wrapping his arm tightly around my shoulders as he ushered me inside. Subtly, so no one would notice, he whispered in my ear, "Do not leave my side, Chloe. Understand me?"

I nodded. I'd been fighting with him all day, but now that we were here, I had no intention of arguing. We went to the bar where Sam ordered us two domestic beers in bottles, exchanging a few words with the bartender. I hated domestic beer, but it didn't look like there was any other option. I knew better than to ask for wine.

The pool hall didn't look anything like I'd imagined. I didn't really know what to expect, but I'd had a picture in my head of the pool table we'd had growing up, with its dark green felt and polished wooden frame. More of those and maybe someplace for people to sit, some couches and chairs.

Balls and Sticks was nothing like that. A dank, acrid haze of smoke hung in the air. The tables were made of plastic and metal, the felt damaged and uneven. The cues looked ancient and warped. The floor was concrete, cracked in places, and far from clean. Light years from clean.

A few people were sitting at the bar, and here and there along the far wall there were stools pulled up to ledges for bottles of beer and ash trays. But mostly, men were standing, playing pool or watching others play pool. There were a few women, but none of them looked like me. I saw one who had bleached blond hair with inches of dark roots, a cigarette handing out of her mouth and an orangey spray tan. In the back, a woman was wrapped around a man, whispering in his ear while he slipped his hand up her shirt. I looked away.

Balls and Sticks was definitely a guy's pool hall. And a lot of them were staring at me. I still didn't get it. The other women here were showing a lot more skin. Nervous, and inwardly cursing my brother for getting me into this in the first place, I turned to lean into Sam, tucking my head into his shoulder.

"Now what?" I asked. He wrapped his free arm tightly around me and said in a low voice,

"What do you mean? I thought you had a plan, honey."

"Sam," I said, willing to admit I was in over my head. "Seriously, how do we find Feliks?"

I knew he was laughing at me after the way I'd insisted we come here and now was hiding in his chest, asking for help. But I wasn't the most outgoing woman, and while the idea of coming in here and demanding to see Feliks had seemed like a good plan in my head, now that I was faced with a room full of strange men who all seemed to be staring at my breasts, I was terrified. Shit.

Sam held me tighter and whispered, "The plan is that you drink your beer. We've got the next open table, and I asked about Feliks."

"When?" I stared up at him.

"When I got our beers."

"Is he here?"

"The bartender didn't say. We'll hang out for a while and if he doesn't show, we go home."

I didn't say anything. I wasn't crazy about that plan. It seemed too passive. But I wasn't going to leave Sam's side to interrogate every man in the place, so I was stuck with it. I knew I was being a wimp, but most of these guys were creepy. There was a lot of long stringy hair, too many missing teeth, and way too many leering gazes for me to feel good about wandering around by myself. Not that Sam would let me. His arm around me gave no question as to whom I belonged.

Our beers were almost empty when a short, skinny man sidled up beside Sam and asked "you look for Feliks?" He had a low, accented voice that sounded too deep to belong to such a narrow body. Sam nodded once and waited. The man's eyes moved to me and he said,

"So, here I am. Who is asking?"

"Do you know Nolan Henson?" I asked. Feliks's eyes narrowed.

"Maybe. Who is asking?"

"I'm his sister. He's missing and-"

"Yeah, I know he's missing," Feliks said, the words choking out on a laugh. "Missing or running is what they say."

"Tell us what you know," Sam said, cutting in.

"For what?"

"Some of this, if what you have is any good," Sam said.

Feliks's eyes fell to Sam's hand and gleamed at the sight of folded bills. Sam was so much better at this getting-information-stuff than I was. It hadn't even occurred to me that I'd need money. Again, I cursed my brother for putting me here in the first place.

"I'll talk to you. For that." Feliks shot his eyes to the money in Sam's hand. "But only if she plays with me."

Sam's eyes went dangerously hard, and the man back peddled. "Pool. She plays a game of pool."

A shot of icy adrenaline tinged fear went through me. He wanted to play me at pool? Here? I didn't want to do it. I didn't want to move from the safety of Sam's arms and go out in the middle of the room with all these men watching and play pool against this creepy guy who might know where my brother was.

But I *could* do it. I was good at pool. Really good. I'd grown up playing all the time at home. It was one of the few things my father would do with us, so Nolan and I both played a lot in the hopes that he would join in and notice that we were there.

The worst thing that could happen was that I'd lose and we'd know what we knew now. Nothing. But if I won… Before Sam could open his mouth to answer, I said, "I'm in."

CHAPTER TWELVE
Sam

My heart stopped for a second when Chloe said yes. It took everything I had to stop myself from dragging her out of the place. But if I did she'd never forgive me. And the table that was opening up for us was close to the door. If the Russian guy had tried to lead us deeper into the pool hall, I might have dragged her out anyway. More than half the men in there were armed and most of them were looking at her like she was fresh meat and they were starving.

Chloe was the best looking women in that room by far. Probably the hottest woman who's ever crossed the threshold. As I walked her to the table, I kissed her temple and said "be careful."

I was assuming she knew how to play pool. Feliks was counting on her desperation to find her brother to goad her into playing, but I knew her. She'd answered with too much confidence for a woman who'd been scared shitless a few minutes ago. My Chloe was going to clean the floor with this guy. Then we could find out what he knew about Nolan, and we'd get the hell out of there.

I didn't have any question in my mind why Feliks would want to kill some time playing pool with Chloe. For one thing, he probably thought it would be funny to mess with her, to take advantage of her clear concern over Nolan and watch her squirm in the hopes that he had useful information, which I doubted.

But that was only part of it. The real answer was that no man, unless he was gay, would pass on the chance to see Chloe bent over a pool table. Either way, I already knew the view would be a killer. Between those tight jeans and the scoop neck shirt, the whole place was about to get a show.

I gritted my teeth and reminded myself that she wanted to do this. She hadn't missed the looks she was getting. She had to know she would draw attention, and I knew it wasn't attention she wanted. Yet she'd jumped to say yes in the hopes she'd find out something useful about Nolan. I was going to back her up even if it killed me.

No one would get to touch her. I knew that. More importantly, she knew that. I didn't have any definite plans to shoot anyone, but my gun was loaded, and if we got into trouble I'd have no problem using it. But I doubted it would come to that.

Watching Chloe select a cue stick, her eyes assessing and knowledgeable, I didn't think the game was going to last long.

I was right. Chloe shyly offered to let Felix break, then took over the table. It was almost worth enduring the greedy leers of the crowd to watch my sweet, beautiful girl destroy the weaselly little Russian.

His break was pathetic, leaving half the balls clumped at the far and of the table. Without comment, without even looking at Feliks, she walked around the table, surveying the placement of the balls. Then she struck, leaning over to sink the first ball, a stripe, with an efficient, direct stroke of the cue. It was almost as beautiful as the sight of her top gaping down to display her breasts, creamy and lush, spilling out of the black lace bra she wore.

My dick went rock hard so fast my head spun. Fuck. Fuck. Fuck. Fuck. I planted my feet on the concrete floor and glared at every other man in the pool hall, aware I couldn't kill them for staring at her breasts. And I couldn't force her to leave. She had to do this, and I had to let her. I reminded myself of that about fifty times between her first shot and her second.

In the minute since Chloe had bent over the table the two nearest games had stopped, the players coming over to watch Chloe and Feliks. My glare intensified until I was surprised laser beams weren't shooting from my eyes.

She rounded the table to stand in front of me and bent over to take her third shot. The sight of her gorgeous ass in those tight jeans almost made me groan. I had a very brief fantasy of fucking her over the pool table at my house before I dragged my attention back to the room.

Her job was to play the game so we could talk to Feliks and then leave. My job was to keep her safe. Thinking with my dick was not going to keep her safe. I could imagine all the ways I was going to fuck her later. Resolved, I kept my eyes off her lush body and kept them on the room.

The other men stayed back. They must have sensed that I was on a hair trigger. It was early, and the crowd wasn't drunk enough to ignore their danger. Or they were struck dumb by the beauty of Chloe running a pool table. She missed her fourth shot after leaning over at a side angle that sent her shirt sliding off one smooth, golden shoulder.

I swore again silently, trying to watch the room without registering the hungry eyes of her observers. Feliks sank two balls and missed a third, but she got her fifth and a very tricky bank shot on the sixth before the Russian got his turn again. The sight of her was murder. Those spike heels, her curvy legs, her perfect round ass. When she planted her feet and spread her legs to shoulder width as she bent over to shoot, I shuddered. I was in hell and she had no idea what she was doing.

Finally, after Feliks sank one more and missed the next, Chloe finished the game, sinking the eight ball on a bank shot that was so precise and cleanly executed I almost wanted to cry.

When the game was done there were a few calls for next game, but Chloe cut them off herself, sending the room her shy smile and saying, "Sorry, that was a one-time thing. But thanks."

Only Chloe could send a bunch of rough guys off with little more than a smile. I think they were all so confused by what a girl like her was doing there in the first place, no one thought to push her. That or they were very sure I'd shoot them if they did. The sweet drained from her face as she turned to pin Feliks to the wall with a glare of her own.

"Okay. We played. Now tell me where my brother is," she demanded.

"Hey, hey," Feliks said, backing up a few steps and raising his hands in front of him. "Keep your voice quiet. I don't want to talk to the whole room."

"Fine," she said in a lower tone. "Where is Nolan?"

"I don't know where Nolan is. I can only tell you what he's been doing."

"And?" I cut in, getting pissed at this guy. He'd gotten what he'd wanted. Now it was Chloe's turn. "Spill it so we can go."

Ignoring me, Feliks looked at Chloe and said "you brother, he used to play some pool with me. I found out what he did, and I hooked him up with my cousin for some work."

"What kind of work?" Chloe asked. Feliks shrugged and mimed typing on a keyboard.

"Hacking stuff," he said. "I don't know what it was. Sergey put him to work."

"Sergey?" I asked, my gut turning to lead. What were the odds this was another Sergey? I'd never been a big believer in coincidence. Feliks's eyes sharpened on my face and I realized that most of his attitude had been an act. He was far sharper than he looked. In a voice so quiet I had to strain to hear, he said,

"Her brother is smart. And not so smart. Like the sister. She should stay home and let the brother find himself. Lot of people looking for him. All bad. Word is, he stole from my cousin."

"Did he?" I asked. Feliks shrugged as if he didn't care or didn't know. "Sergey looking for him, too. A pretty woman should stay home. Out of the way."

He raised his grizzled eyebrows, asking me if I understood. I did. We were getting the fuck out of there, and I was going to do my best to convince Chloe to leave the rest of this in Axel's hands. If Nolan was working for Tsepov, I wanted Chloe nowhere near him.

CHAPTER THIRTEEN
Chloe

Sam's jaw was tight as he drove back to his house. He looked pissed off and I couldn't tell if he was mad at me, Nolan, both of us, or the whole situation. Probably the last. I wanted to tell him he didn't have to worry about it, that I appreciated his help, but I could handle this on my own. I wasn't stupid. I could imagine what might have happened if I'd walked into Balls and Sticks alone. I needed Sam's help.

"Who is Sergey?" I asked, needing to know. Sam had reacted to the name as if it had meant something to him.

"I'm guessing it's Tsepov."

"The Russian mob guy? The one with the poker room where Tim said Nolan was playing?"

"Yes." Sam flicked his eyes to me. In the dark, they gleamed a hard, deep blue. "And no. You are not going anywhere near that poker room or Tsepov.

I'll call Axel when I get home and see what he's got. But you're staying out of this."

"Sam, I think-" He cut me off before I could say anything else.

"No. Just no. I get that you need to help find your brother. But if Nolan loves you anywhere near as much as you love him, do you really think he wants you getting tangled up with the Russian mob?"

"No," I said. Then, in a small voice, I admitted, "If he was really thinking of me at all, he wouldn't have gotten involved with them, either."

Sam took my hand and squeezed. It was no more than he'd been trying to point out for a while. Nolan lived with me. If he'd been across town, or in another city, things would have been different. But when we shared an address, anything he brought home was tied to me. He'd put me in danger. And for what? Why? With a sigh, I looked out the window and let my thoughts drift. I wanted a break, just for a little while. I didn't want to think about Nolan. I didn't want to worry.

Sam parked the car in the garage and came around to help me out. Like he had the day before, instead of giving me his hand, he slid his arm around my back and lifted me out, pressing my body into his. At the impact of his hard chest, my nipples beaded into points and I let out a tiny gasp. I wasn't a small woman, but Sam was so big next to me, tall and all muscle.

I tried not to whimper as he lowered me, scraping my nipples against his chest, the impact barely dulled by our clothes. Just before my feet touched the concrete, he swore and lifted me again, raising me to waist height. My legs instinctively locked around his waist in a tight clasp, holding him to my body.

With a groan, he pressed me into the side of his truck as his mouth came down on mine. My sensible side was nowhere to be found. I opened for him, my lips warming under his, my tongue reaching into his mouth. His kiss stole my breath away as I fell into it, sinking my hands into his hair and gripping tight to keep him exactly where he was.

Sam's hips pinned me to the side of the truck, and I felt the hard length of his cock pressing through layers of denim to tease me. I couldn't help but rock my hips into the delicious friction. When his hand snaked under my shirt to splay across my back, I shivered from the heat and strength in his fingers. A twist of those fingers on the clasp of my bra and the band fell loose.

He didn't hesitate in leaning me forward to get to my breasts, and I was too far gone to stop him. His hands now more frantic than practiced, he leaned me back into the truck and pushed my shirt up, dragging my bra with it, until my breasts were exposed in the dimly lit garage.

"Fuck, Chloe. I swear you're the most perfect thing I've ever seen," he groaned. I might have doubted him, but the look in his eyes, the hunger and rapt devotion convinced me that, whatever I thought, Sam loved my breasts. Before I could think about what he was doing, he dropped his mouth to one nipple and sucked.

My head fell back with the shock of hot pleasure, thunking against the truck's frame. I moaned and arched my back, offering him more. With the press of his hips and the clasp of my legs holding me up, Sam had both hands free, and he used them. Strong fingers closed over my breast, plumping it, feeding my nipple into his mouth as he sucked harder, then shifted his head to feast on the other side.

I rocked against him, the pressure between my legs sending me higher, flooding my body with more pleasure than I'd ever felt from a man, more than I'd dreamed in those times I'd slid my own fingers between my legs and imagined what it would be like with Sam.

"Sam," I moaned, as his fingers closed over one nipple and he tongued the other. "Sam, please. Please."

I didn't even know what I was asking for. Not really. But the promise of his mouth on my breasts was shredding my intentions. All my protests about a relationship with Sam had drifted away, dispersed by this dizzying pleasure and the reality of being touched, not by a man, but by Sam.

Who knows how far it would have gone if his

phone hadn't begun to ring. At first we ignored it, too lost in our desire for one another to care about the insistent beeping in Sam's pocket. When the phone fell silent and then began to sound again, Sam groaned and pulled away, drawing a moan of disappointment from between my lips.

Still, he ignored the phone, gently pulling down my shirt, his eyes not meeting mine. He answered the phone, his arm around my shoulders firmly leading me past the hood of the truck and into the back hall of the house.

"What do you have?" A pause. "I'll call you back when I'm in my office. Give me a minute."

Sam walked me to his bedroom door and stopped. His eyes touched on mine, then skated away, their normally vibrant blue dark and shadowed.

"Chloe," he said and stopped. "I-"

"Sam, it's-"

"No," he said, interrupting. "Don't tell me it's okay. I promised you I wasn't going to push you. Or take advantage. And I'm not. I won't. I'm not going to change your mind like this. I'm sorry. Go to bed. I'll see you in the morning."

Without letting me say a word, he left, walking across the hall to his office and closing the door behind him. Deflated, and a little confused, I went into his room and did the same. Leaning back into the heavy door, I stared at Sam's room with blind eyes. It looked wrong without him in it.

Something deep in my heart hummed at the thought. He should be here with me. This was wrong. My protests, though they'd been well intentioned, were wrong. I shook my head, trying to drive the idea away. It wasn't the time to think about Sam. Not while Nolan was still missing and the rest of my life was upside down. I was under too much stress to consider making a choice that could ruin my life.

With nothing else to do, I went to the bathroom and turned on the shower. I'd taken one that morning, but the stale scent of cigarette smoke clung to my skin. Skin that still hummed from the arousal Sam's kiss had begun. It looked like I wasn't going to see how much better it could get. At least not any time soon. Resigned to a night alone, I climbed in the shower to clean up before I tried to sleep. Perversely, I used Sam's body wash/shampoo instead of my own soap, wanting to smell him on my skin if I couldn't feel his touch.

I brushed my teeth and dried my hair without thinking about it, my mind turning over the past day, trying to fit together the pieces of what was going on, both with Nolan and between Sam and myself. So much was changing, so much unknown. I felt adrift. And I wanted Sam.

Crawling into bed, I tried to sleep. My mind and my body refused. My body was still wound up, tense from worry and unfulfilled desire. My mind refused to settle, insisting over and over, no matter how I tried to work around it, that I needed to be with Sam. I couldn't tell if I was trying to talk myself into it because my body desperately wanted the orgasm that had been hovering out of reach as he'd sucked my nipples, or if I truly had moved past my fear of a relationship with him.

None of my concerns had changed. If he decided to move on, I'd lose my best friend, my job, and my heart. It was too much to risk. But if it worked, every dream I'd ever had would come true.

With a frustrated growl, I turned over and punched my pillow. I'd chosen one of the nightgowns Lola had sent over, a mid-thigh length cream silk trimmed in pink lace. It was soft and silky on my skin, the slide of the fabric as I moved only reminding me that I was alone when I should be with Sam.

This was why I'd insisted he not try to seduce me. He was as bad as that piece of chocolate cake I saw at the bakery and ended up buying. I knew I shouldn't have it, but one look, one memory of how good it was, and I convinced myself I needed it. Except that Sam was so much better than the best chocolate cake I'd ever had. And that was saying something. I loved chocolate cake.

Eventually, I broke. Had he known this would happen? That once he got his hands on me I'd lose the ability to say no? I shoved the covers back and got out of bed, storming for the door, so frustrated and annoyed I wasn't sure if I planned to jump on Sam or yell at him.

I didn't get the chance to do either. When I swung open the door to his office, it was empty. A quick search of the rest of the house showed the same. Sam was gone.

the Courtship Maneuver

BOOK TWO

CHAPTER ONE
Chloe

I had a pretty good idea where Sam was. 315 Studen Street, trying to find a man named Dog in a poker room. Fury bloomed in my chest, driving out my arousal and frustration. He couldn't set me aside and then leave. He wanted me to stay home like a good girl and follow orders. What had that gotten me? Alone and frustrated. Forget that.

I knew I was being unreasonable. And I wasn't going to be foolish. But I didn't want to be left out, either. Now that my head was clear of passion, if not anger, I realized that the phone call earlier must have been Axel. They'd gone to the poker room without me. But I had my car and GPS. They wouldn't be that hard to find.

Before I could think better of it, I went to the closet looking for something to wear. Not jeans. I found a dress that I hadn't noticed that morning. A very dark, fine denim, cut in a wrap style. It was sexy, but not formal. Perfect for a bar. At least, I thought it was. I knew the bars I'd been to hadn't had poker rooms in the back, so this was yet another situation where I had no idea what I was getting into.

Warning bells clanged in the back of my head. *Danger! Danger! Danger!* I ignored them. Anger swelled and grew in my chest until tears welled in my eyes. He'd kissed me senseless, touched me like I'd never been touched before, and then sent me to bed like a child. I wasn't a child. I was a *woman*. And I had a right to make my own decisions.

The small part of me that was still rational called bullshit on my reasoning. I had a right to make my own decisions, it insisted, but this one was stupid. I ignored it. Pulling on the dress over the black lace bra and panties I'd worn earlier, I slipped on wedge sandals that went with the dress and checked the whole thing in the bathroom mirror.

My reflection took me aback. My normally cheerful brown eyes blazed with outrage. My round cheeks were flushed a dark pink. Ignoring yet another warning sign that I was emotional and not thinking clearly, I dragged a brush through my hair, then deliberately picked up my eyeliner and began to make up my face with more attention than usual.

When I was ready, I grabbed my purse and keys from the dresser and headed for the garage, typing the address into my phone's GPS app as I went, my ever-growing fury propelling me at a brisk pace. I was over halfway to Stubens Street before I started to wonder what the hell I was doing.

Unlike the trip to the pool hall, this one wasn't taking me into the scarier areas of Vegas. I was twisting and turning through downtown when the GPS indicated I'd arrived. The street was a mix of old and new, the bar I was looking for one of the older establishments, and the only one I could see that had its own parking lot.

I turned into the lot slowly, the alarm bells in my head clanging louder with every second that passed. Or maybe my fury had faded enough that I could hear them now, echoing in my skull in insistent demand that I stop and think before I did anything else. Trying to be sensible, I dialed Sam on my phone. Maybe he wasn't even here, I reasoned. I hadn't checked the lot for his truck yet, but maybe I'd misread the whole thing and I could turn around and go home.

The phone at my ear rang five times before it rolled over to voice mail. I put it down and drove in a circle until I found a parking space. Right beside Sam's truck. That bastard. Inwardly, I fumed. I'd been on the edge of giving up and going home, but the sight of Sam's oversized midnight blue truck set me off again. He was here. Either alone or with Axel, he'd left me at home alone to stew while he came here to find out more about the mess Nolan had gotten himself into.

Was I really going to do this? It was one thing to sit in the car and be pissed at Sam, but I had no idea what the bar would be like. It could be the pool hall all over again. On this street it could go either way and I wouldn't know until I was inside. But Sam was in there. And so was a man who knew more about Nolan and where he could be. My resolve wavering, I sat in the car for another moment, balanced on the edge of decision. Go in or go home? Go in or go home?

I teetered for another moment before I crashed to one side, knowing what I had to do and scared to death about doing it.

CHAPTER TWO
Sam

Axel gave me a look and shook his head, already annoyed with the man called Dog. He was a big guy, not Russian, but according to him, another cousin of Sergey Tsepov. I wasn't sure I believed that. So far, most of what had come out of Dog's mouth sounded like bullshit. Nothing here was what I'd expected when Axel said we'd be going to check out the poker room.

I played cards from time to time, but I wasn't into it enough to have sat a game in a place like this. Axel had. He had skills at poker, enough that he could have made a living with it if he'd wanted to. Over the years he'd hit most of the rooms in town at least once. Not this one, though. It was new and Axel had been more focused on business than fun for the last few years. He'd played some tournaments, but his days of pulling all nighters in high-stakes games were over.

I'd thought the bar in front of a poker room would be a lot like the pool hall we'd been in earlier. Some of them probably were, but this place was a step up. Far up. It had the look of a gentleman's club, and not the kind with dancers. Old school, a club intended to appeal to gentlemen looking to relax and just be men for the night. Polished wood floors, dark leather couches and armchairs, generously poured drinks, and plenty of visible yet discreet flat screens, each showing a different game.

If I hadn't known who owned it, I might've wanted to hang out here myself. But I'd learned to steer clear of anything connected to Tsepov. Despite the appealing atmosphere and the high quality whiskey in my glass, I didn't want to be sitting with Axel trying to drag information out of Dog. I wanted to be home with Chloe.

I couldn't decide if it was a good thing or bad that Axel called when he had. My dick was voting for bad. Fuck, but Chloe had been hot. I'd kissed a lot of women. Maybe too many. Not a single one had been as good as Chloe.

She caught fire in my arms, and either she was too inexperienced or she didn't care, but she never tried to hide her response to me. It was intoxicating. I'd been hard since the pool hall. Feeling her grind against me as she yanked my face into her full, soft breasts almost made me come in my pants like a teenager.

I had no idea what would've happened if phone hadn't rung. That's a lie. I would've fucked her. The only question was would I have done it standing up against the side of my truck, or would I have been able to wait until I got her into the house?

My conscience was calling me an asshole. Just that morning, I'd promised her I wouldn't push. That hadn't lasted long. I meant the promise when I gave it. Shit, I still meant it. But she'd been right -- just touching her was taking advantage when she didn't have the experience to handle the way I made her feel. In my defense, I'd never had a woman who responded to me so perfectly. She was addicting.

It wasn't just that she was gorgeous, lush and curvy and sweet and soft. But she was Chloe. My confidant, my partner, the only real female friend I'd ever had. All of that in such a hot package? I wasn't surprised I was having a hard time keeping my head straight.

I had to keep my hands off her. Somehow. If I was going to prove to Chloe that she could trust me to take care with her, I had to actually take care *with* her. Though fuck, it had been hard to let her play that game of pool against the little Russian and not start a fight with every man in the room who was appreciating her tits and ass as much as I was.

Beside me, Axel stiffened and glanced at the door. Dog sat across the table telling a useless story about a poker game where he'd gone heads-up against Nolan and taken all the kid's money. I had the feeling he knew something we could use, but like Feliks, he was playing dumb. I couldn't tell if it was out of self-preservation or just to fuck with us. It didn't matter. Both Axel and I were starting to lose patience.

Now Axel had shifted in his seat so he had a clear view of the front door. Not wanting to be obvious, I kept my eyes on Dog, but something was up and I wanted to know what it was. A moment later Axel swore under his breath. I gave into temptation and checked the door myself.

For the first time in my entire life, my head came close to actually exploding. Chloe stood just inside the heavy, carved wooden doors, clutching her purse in front of her and scanning the room with nervous eyes as the tall, wide bouncer blocked her way. There weren't many women in the bar, and I realized at that moment that all of them were with a man.

Clearly this was not an establishment that welcomed women alone. Though the way Chloe was dressed, in her not-quite-casual, not-quite-formal deep blue wrap dress and matching sandals, she was a perfect fit for the place. The sight of her was killing me. The dress fit her generous curves to perfection, showing off her shapely legs and full breasts without being obvious. And sometime between when I'd heard her shower go on and when she'd left, she'd done something to her hair that left it smooth and shiny against her shoulders. She was wearing makeup, too. More than usual, and it was expertly applied to make her normally warm brown eyes look exotic. Almost dangerous.

Or maybe that was her temper. She scowled at the bouncer, said something we couldn't hear, and started forward. The bouncer shifted and put an arm out to stop her. Axel leaned toward me and said,

"I'm going to go get her. We don't want her causing a scene and I don't think she's going to leave quietly."

All I could say was "fuck."

Across from me, Dog finally realized we weren't paying attention to his story and looked up. Axel rose and crossed the room to the door. His eyebrows shot up when he caught sight of Chloe.

"Your woman track you down?" he asked in a scornful tone that said he thought less of a man whose woman would come out to find him.

I didn't respond. I wanted Chloe off the radar. By coming here she'd jumped square into the middle of the clusterfuck surrounding her brother. Anything I said to Dog would give him information I didn't want him to have. I watched as Axel took Chloe's arm and the bouncer stepped back to let them pass.

Axel dropped his head and whispered something in her ear. Her eyes narrowed, focused on me, and for a second I was the target of her furious glare. A moment later the expression melted from her face and she smiled serenely Axel.

Relief and worry warred inside me. It seemed Chloe was going to play along and behave herself, which was the only good option if she had to be here at all. But I wasn't just worried about how pissed she seemed to be at me. I didn't like her exposure to Dog and whoever else might be watching.

I stood when she approached, sliding my chair over to make room for the one Axel slid beside it. Chloe sat, her eyes on Dog, and didn't acknowledge me. I waited for her to speak. Dog seemed to be waiting for an introduction. Both of us were disappointed.

CHAPTER THREE
Chloe

It took all of my courage just to get out of the car. I lost my nerve twice before I finally opened the door. As I walked around the corner from the parking lot to the front door of the bar, my heart pounded in my chest so hard I could hear it in my ears. The doors themselves were intimidating, thick and tall, the wood heavily carved in patterns I didn't recognize. Even the handles seem designed to scare me off, large unpolished brass meant for a man's hands, too big for mine.

Once I was inside, it didn't get any better. A glance told me the bar was not what I'd expected. I don't really know what I thought it was going to be like, maybe scruffier with bad lighting and peanut shells on the floor. Instead, the dark colors and heavy leather furniture reminded me of my father's office. So did the smell of cigar smoke and whiskey, comforting and sad at the same time. Then I spotted Axel and Sam in the far corner and all of my emotions but anger faded away.

I would've marched right across the place and lit into Sam but for two things. Sam and Axel seemed to be talking to someone, a big man with dark hair and ruddy cheeks. And a man in a dark suit had stepped in front of me the moment the door shut, politely yet firmly refusing me entrance.

"I'm sorry miss," he said. "You may not come in without a companion."

I looked up at him in shock. What was he talking about? Wasn't it illegal to refuse entrance to a public space based on my gender?

"Is this a private club?" I asked. His eyes narrowed on my face.

"It is."

"Well then how did my friends get in?" I asked, nodding my head in Axel and Sam's direction.

As I spoke, Axel looked up and over his shoulder, spotting me instantly. The expression on his face was not reassuring. I'd known Axel for a few years. He was miserly in showing his emotions. Tonight was no different. Unfortunately I knew him well enough to be able to read the tightness in his jaw and the angle of his eyebrows as utter fury.

Well, too bad for him. And for Sam, too. I was here, and I wasn't leaving until I knew something about my brother, something that would help me find him. Sam must've read Axel's look, because he turned in his seat, and his face when he saw me would have been picture worthy if I wanted any memory of Sam that incredulously angry.

Turning my attention back to the bouncer, I said, "Well, may I go join my friends?"

He gave a short shake of his head and shifted to block my way once again. "They are our guests for the evening," he said. "You may join them if one of them comes to get you."

"Well, tell them I'm here then," I said, trying to muster every ounce of confidence I had. It wasn't much, and the bouncer knew it.

"I am sorry miss, but they have already seen you. You must wait to see if they will come for you." He gave a deliberately obvious look at his wristwatch and then back at me. I had the sudden urge to stomp my sandaled foot. I still wasn't sure this was exactly legal even if he was claiming the bar was a private club.

My chest loosened with relief when Axel rose and headed our way. He barely acknowledged me as he took my arm with a nod to the bouncer and led me back to their table. All he said was, "Keep your mouth shut and let me talk, Chloe. Do you understand?"

Sam met my eyes as we walked closer and I couldn't help the glare that escaped. Knowing that a tantrum would only get in the way of finding out about Nolan, I reined in my emotions and smiled up at Axel with the sweetest, most compliant expression

I could muster. I saw in his eyes that he wasn't buying it, but was at least relieved that I was going to play along.

I sat in the chair he pulled out for me, pretending to ignore Sam, which was nearly impossible, considering how every cell in my body woke up the moment I was close to him. But I was still too pissed off to know what to say. This was neither the time nor the place to begin the argument we'd have the second we were alone.

Axel, apparently done with hanging around now that I was there, focused his attention on the big, red-faced man sitting opposite us and said, "So let's get into it. Do you know where Nolan Henson is?"

The man's gaze sharpened. "I already told you, I have no idea where Nolan Henson is. Did you think that if you brought his sister here I would soften up and tell you?"

I drew in an audible breath. I'd never seen this man before in my life. How did he know who I was? Nolan occasionally had friends over to our apartment, but not this man. I would have remembered him. There was something about him, something off, as if he were lying or playing a part and not doing it terribly well. I didn't understand enough about what was going on to know if my instinct was accurate or if it was just my own nerves making me jumpy.

"How do you know who she is?" Axel asked.

"Nolan talked about his sister Chloe all the time,"

the man said. "What a good sister she was, even when she nagged him to clean up his room or eat his vegetables with his dinner." He smirked at me as if laughing at my concerns. "But he never mentioned how beautiful she is." His eyes raked over me and I wished, for the first time since I'd tried on the clothes Lola had chosen for me, that I was wearing the suit Sam had thrown away.

Sam shifted beside me, saying nothing, but the waves of coiled menace that rolled off him were enough. Dog must have thought so too because after a quick look in Sam's direction he refocused his attention on Axel.

"Chloe isn't what's important here," Axel said. "When was the last time you saw Nolan?"

"I saw him Saturday," Dog said.

"Were you with him before he disappeared?" Axel asked.

"Not right before, no. The last person who saw Nolan before he disappeared is dead."

I gasped and straightened in my chair. Was he implying Nolan had killed someone? I bit my tongue hard to keep from asking questions. Axel asked them for me.

"What are you saying?"

"Look, normally I wouldn't talk about any of this outside the family," the man said leaning forward, bracing his elbows on his knees. "But I can tell you three are going to cause trouble until you find out what you want to know, and that isn't going to help anybody."

For the first time since I walked in, Sam spoke. "So why don't you just talk and we'll get out of your way."

"Nolan has been working for Sergey," Dog finally said. "He was given a job. To-" A pause, "acquire some information from a competitor. Very valuable information. As far as we know, he acquired this information. In the process, one of the competitor's men turned up dead and Nolan is nowhere. Neither is the information. Believe me when I tell you there are a lot of people who would like to know where your brother is."

He said this last part staring at me. I stared back, my eyes wide with horror. So not only was my brother missing, he'd gone missing while committing a crime for a Russian mob boss and possibly killing someone? I wanted to run screaming from the room, denying that Nolan could have done any of it. After the last few days I wished I was still naïve enough to believe him that innocent. It was going to take a lot to convince me he killed anyone, but the rest - hacking information for Sergey Tsepov and then messing up somehow and running away? It hurt my heart how easily I could believe that part was true.

"Chloe, describe to Dog the men you saw in your apartment," Axel said in a low voice. I did as best I could remember. When I described the tall man with the heavy accent who'd had the gun, I would have sworn I saw recognition flicker in Dogs eyes, but he said,

"They don't sound like anyone I know. But a lot of people are looking for Nolan. Who knows who they could be?"

"And does Tsepov think Nolan is holding the information to sell it himself?" Axel asked. Dog shrugged as if he either didn't know or didn't care.

"Sergey likes his little pet. He doesn't believe Nolan has the balls to double-cross him. But he will find him either way. And if he can prove that Nolan tried to betray him-"

Dog shrugged again, clearly not concerned about my brother's fate. My stomach rolled. For a few seconds my mouth flooded with saliva, and I thought I was going to throw up. I had no idea what a Russian mob boss would do to an underling he thought had betrayed him. I was sure that whatever punishment I could dream up, Tsepov's would be worse.

Sam and Axel both stood at once, Sam taking my arm in his as he did, pulling me to my feet beside him. Axel handed Dog a business card and said, "If you hear anything, It's worth something to let me know."

Dog gave the card a brief look and set it on the table beside his drink. I doubted we'd be hearing from him. He had his loyalty, and it wasn't to Nolan's family.

With a steely grip on my elbow, Sam half led, half dragged me out of the bar. He propelled me straight to his truck, his silence heavy. Before I could mention it he said to Axel, "Get someone to bring Chloe's car back."

Axel's answer was, "Keys?"

I thought about arguing, but the look in Sam's eyes convinced me to let him have his way. I pulled my car keys out of my purse and handed them to Sam who tossed them across the parking lot to Axel. Opening the truck door, he lifted me in and watched, hands on his hips, while I fastened my seatbelt. Did he think I was going to make a break for it? We were in the middle of a dark parking lot in the middle of downtown Vegas and I didn't even have my own car keys.

Sam was in the car, engine running, when I opened my mouth to speak. I didn't get out a sound before he raised his hand to stop me, saying "so help me, Chloe, do not say a single word until we are home and behind a locked door. I guarantee you I will be a lot more reasonable once I know you're somewhere safe."

With a huff, I sat back in my seat, mouth closed. Not because he'd told me to be quiet. I had plenty to say, and I was going to say it. No, I kept my mouth shut because when I started yelling at Sam I didn't want to have to worry about him watching the road. I wanted his full attention so I could make sure he understood how completely furious I was. Unfortunately, I had a feeling Sam was thinking the exact same thing.

CHAPTER FOUR
Chloe

I followed Sam into the house, down the hall from the garage, and into the kitchen where he whirled on me, his eyes so angry they shot blue sparks. "What the fuck were you thinking, Chloe?" he shouted. "Do you have any fucking idea what you just fucking did?"

"If it was that dangerous," I asked, "what were you doing there? If it was that bad, shouldn't you have let Axel handle it?"

"Are you fucking kidding me?" Sam asked, his face openly disbelieving.

"No, I'm not kidding you. Tell me how it's different. And watch your language," I snapped.

"I will not watch my fucking language. It's different in a thousand ways, Chloe. But do you want to know the most important one? Those guys have no interest in me. I'm just asking questions about a problem. Most likely, they don't want me asking those questions, but that's fine. They won't run the risk of fucking with me because I'm too well-known, and I've got too much money to make it worth getting me interested in their shit. But you? You're a beautiful, desirable, and very inexperienced woman stumbling in the middle of a shit storm she doesn't understand."

"What exactly don't I understand?" I crossed my arms over my chest. I knew I wasn't worldly, but I wasn't completely naïve. Sam was making me sound useless and stupid, which was only pissing me off more.

"What you don't understand," Sam said his voice level and deadly, "is that you are not a *person* to men like that. You are a commodity to be bought, sold, or traded for something else of value. Beautiful women fall into their hands every day and are never heard from again."

"Bought, sold, or traded? They *sell* women?" I asked, confused. I thought that was movie of the week stuff. I didn't think it really happened.

"Tsepov personally owns three brothels. Two of them are above board. One of them defines sketchy. I've heard things about the way the women cycle through his houses. Stories that some of his girls are not there by choice. And when there are that many rumors, Chloe, there's usually truth. And now you've been in his bar. I guaran-fucking-tee you he had surveillance on our table. So now he knows who you are.

What you look like. You're on his radar, which is the last place you should be."

"Oh," I said, at a complete loss for words. Of all the things I thought he'd be upset about, me being a victim of human trafficking had not been on the list. "You left without telling me. I went to your office, and you weren't there."

"THEN YOU SHOULD HAVE JUST GONE BACK TO BED!" Sam yelled.

"Stop shouting, you'll wake up your Dad." I hissed at him, suddenly remembering that Daniel was somewhere in the house. It was a big place, and his rooms were on another level, but the last thing I wanted, or needed, was another overprotective male wandering into this conversation.

"It's my fucking house, I'll shout if I want to," Sam said, at a slightly lower volume than before. Nether of us were doing a very good job at being sensible or reasonable. Between me running off to find him at the bar, which I admitted to myself was a bad idea, and Sam yelling at me over his right to yell, we were both acting like children.

"And watch your language," I unwisely said again.

His eyes flared, and he reached out to grab my arm, dragging me down the hallway that led to his bedroom and office. I had to scramble to keep up, stumbling once in my wedge sandals. When I faltered, Sam kept going, sweeping me up in his arms and tossing me over his shoulder as he had the night before. I hit his back as hard as I could shouting, "PUT ME DOWN! PUT ME DOWN, YOU BASTARD!"

He ignored me completely. Shoving open the door to his room with one booted foot, Sam dumped me back on my feet, and kicked the door shut behind him, catching my arm when my heel twisted beneath me. He stepped away as soon as I was steady, glaring at me.

"Better?" he asked with a sarcastic sneer. "I promise you Dad can't hear anything from my rooms when he's downstairs. I've had plenty of proof. We can be as loud as we want and he won't hear a thing."

I felt the blood drain from my face as I realized what he'd said. He wasn't talking about yelling. At least not in a fight. He was talking about women. All the women he'd fucked in here and not had to worry about how loud they were. Suddenly, our fight seemed ridiculous. A sick ball of regret and pain grew in my stomach, and I sank to the edge of the bed, my eyes on the carpet.

What was I doing? Why had I even gone to the bar?

Because I was mad he'd walked out on me. But that was stupid. We shouldn't have been kissing in the first place. I should have been glad he'd left. Sam wasn't mine. He'd never be mine. First thing in the morning I had to leave here and find somewhere else to stay. Maybe see if I could hire Axel to protect me until we found Nolan. Anything to get away from Sam.

"Chloe," he said, his voice still loud in the suddenly silent room. "That wasn't what I meant. I'm sorry, I was angry and-"

"Just go away Sam," I said, unable to look at him. My lungs were tight and I could feel the beginnings of tears prickling my eyes. I didn't want to cry in front of Sam. "I'm tired and I want to go to sleep."

"No, Chloe. Just look at me. I'm sorry I said that."

"It's fine Sam. I'm fine." I kept my eyes down, my fingers plucking absently at the comforter, waiting for him to go. I didn't recognize my own voice, tight and thick with unshed tears.

"Chloe," he said, getting to his knees in front of me to force me to meet his eyes.

After a moment, I did, and his tortured gaze trapped mine. His face was so pained, I couldn't look away. He took my restless hands in his and held them tightly, rubbing my palms with his thumbs.

"Chloe, I'm sorry. I didn't mean it like that. I was angry. I don't think you understand how much you scared me tonight. You didn't see the way they looked at you. The pool hall was one thing, and letting Feliks see you wasn't good. But he's not even officially working with Tsepov. He's not a real danger. Dog *is*. That bar is more than a front for a poker room, it's one of the places Tsepov uses as a base. He may have been there tonight, watching the whole thing. I can't keep you safe if you throw yourself into danger."

"I didn't know," I whispered. I'd had an idea going to the bar wasn't a great idea, but as far as I'd known, it was just a bar. Maybe it was going to be a little rough, but I didn't know anything about brothels and women forced into selling themselves.

"I didn't know," I said again, feeling low and useless. Not only had I discovered my brother was in far worse trouble than I'd thought, I'd managed to get myself into trouble too. I was a joke, trying to look out for Nolan and me. All I did lately was mess things up worse.

"I didn't tell you," Sam said, trying to catch my eyes again. "I didn't think you'd go there. I wasn't planning to go. I was going to let Axel handle it. But then things got out of control in the garage and I thought it was better if I left for a while."

"I wish you'd said something. If I'd known how bad it would be, I wouldn't have gone, even if I was mad at you."

Sam let go of my hands and braced his palms on either side of my legs. With the difference in our heights and the low bed, his head was almost level with mine even though he was kneeling. He traced one finger down my bare arm and asked,

"You came to find me? Before you left?"

I nodded.

"Why? Did you need something?"

I didn't answer, too embarrassed to admit why I'd gone to find him. Especially after the reminder of how many other women he'd made love to on this bed. Beautiful women. Sexy, skinny, perfect women. I didn't fit with Sam, no matter what he'd said that morning.

"Clo? Tell me."

"I just... I wanted you to-" I froze, unable to say it. Sam stared at me, his eyes on mine, tentative. Hopeful. I don't know where I got the courage. I couldn't find the words to say what I'd wanted. What I still wanted. Instead, I showed him.

CHAPTER FIVE
Chloe

I leaned forward the few inches separating me from Sam and pressed my lips to his. I don't think I'd ever initiated a kiss with a man. Aside from pressing my lips to Sam's, I didn't know what to do. When we'd kissed before, I hadn't put much thought into what I was doing. Forget much thought, I hadn't put any thought into it. Sam had kissed me and my body had taken over.

There was a moment of doubt. That he would reject me, that I was doing it wrong, before Sam groaned and his arms closed around me. His lips took mine, deepening the kiss, his tongue rubbing and tasting in a dance that stole my breath. He rose above me, sliding me onto the bed until I was flat on my back. My legs spread and my knees came up to grip his hips as I felt his weight pinning me down.

His kiss made me crazy. The taste of Sam in my mouth, the citrus and spice scent of him, his big, hard hands, one on my waist and the other on my face. My hips rolled beneath him, my body urging me on, demanding more even though I didn't know how to ask for what I needed. I didn't have to. For the first time I was grateful for Sam's experience. He knew exactly what to do. He just didn't move fast enough.

Breaking our kiss, he sat up, kneeling between my spread legs. His eyes, sharp and hot, raked my body, his breath coming in short pants, exactly like my own.

"Chloe, honey," he said, his voice growly and low. "I need to know that you understand where this is going. That you want this. You have to tell me. I'm not going to take advantage of you."

"I do," I said, squirming beneath him, clamping my knees to his thighs and lifting my hips just a little. I didn't really know what I was doing, or why. I just knew my body needed to move and Sam was so still, watching me. His eyes, flaring every time I shifted, only made me more restless. "Sam, please."

Sam trailed a finger up my leg from my ankle, still wrapped by the sandal strap, up my calf, past my knee to my thigh. I shivered from the deliberate touch. "Have you done this before, Chloe?"

I nodded. "Once," I admitted. Sam's eyes went white hot.

"Just once?" he asked in a tight voice. "How long ago?"

His finger traced circles on my upper thigh, distracting me from his question. I managed to answer, "In college. But I didn't-"

"Shh." Sam's finger left my leg and dropped over my lips. "Was it bad? Did he hurt you?" I shook my head. It hadn't been bad. It just hadn't been good enough to try again.

"Good. This will be different."

I nodded again, eager for Sam to stop talking and get on with it. His erection pressed against his pants, long and thick. He wanted this as much as I did. I didn't want to talk about it. I wanted to touch him. To feel him inside me.

"You want me to make love to you, Chloe? You want me to fuck you?" he asked, his finger gone from my mouth and back on my thigh, this time tracing those teasing circles on the tender, sensitive flesh on the inside, less than six inches above my heated pussy. I wiggled, hoping it would encourage him to slide his fingers a little lower, but he ignored me. "I need you to say it, Clo. I promised you I wouldn't take advantage of you. That I wouldn't do this until you asked. So if you want it, ask me."

"Sam," I whispered, raising my hands to the hidden button between my breasts. "Fuck me. Please."

"You're sure?" he asked, lifting my right foot to his shoulder, stretching my leg straight, the position sending me off balance, leaving me deliciously vulnerable before him. But this was Sam, and I liked being vulnerable to Sam. I could trust him with this.

With precise movements, he unfastened the tiny buckle holding my sandal on my foot and slid it off. He placed my now bare foot on the bed beside his knee and lifted the other leg, slowly and carefully removing that shoe as well.

My breath catching in my chest, I undid the button between my breasts, but left the dress closed. Dropping my hands to my waist, I slipped the other hidden button free and carefully untied the belt that was the only remaining thing holding the dress together. Sam licked his lips, dropping my second sandal on the floor at the end of the bed and gently arranging my foot in the same position as the other. Sucking in a breath for courage, I drew open my dress and bared my almost naked body.

Sam made a choking sound in his throat as he looked at me. I started to get nervous. I wasn't exactly a small woman. And I'd never been naked in front of a man. The one time I'd had sex in college we'd been under the covers in the dark and he hadn't seen anything. This was different.

My whole body was exposed except what was covered by the black lace bra and panties, and they didn't cover much. I started to grab for the edges of the dress, intending to pull it closed, when I saw Sam's hands, hanging by his sides, trembling.

His chest rose and fell as he remained where he was, motionless, kneeling between my legs, his eyes moving over every inch of exposed skin. His tongue came out to lick his lower lip. He blinked. But he didn't move. The almost imperceptible shake of his hands gave me courage.

Sam wasn't disgusted by my body. He wanted me. So much so that he was frozen, waiting to be sure. I couldn't reach the clasp of my bra, so I did the next best thing and pulled down the straps, peeling the lace over my breasts until they were completely bare and sliding to the sides without the bra to hold them up. My nipples beaded into tight knots as his eyes fastened to them. One hand reached out, his fingers almost pinching together before his arm fell back to his side.

Emboldened, I dropped my hands to my hips, wondering what it would take to break Sam free from his immobility. I didn't have to wonder for long. I hooked my thumbs in the sides of the black lace panties and began to work them down my hips when Sam said, his voice hoarse,

"Stop."

I did, the panties caught just above my hips. Sam was off the bed in a flash, standing at the end, gripping my legs behind my knees to drag me toward him until my rear end was almost falling off the mattress. He let my legs dangle and leaned over me, quickly undoing my bra and yanking my dress away until I was truly naked except for my barely on panties.

"Chloe," he said, stroking his hands over my skin, touching my legs, my waist, weighing my breasts and exploring my elbows with equal attention. "Chloe. So perfect. So exactly right. I've been dreaming of this." He pulled my panties off in one swipe, tossing them over his shoulder.

Then he was on his knees, his shoulders pushing my legs wide, his face inches from my pussy. I was exposed, open to him in a way I'd never experienced before. I didn't have time to get scared. His palms came down on my inner thighs, spreading my legs even wider as his mouth dropped between them.

I gasped from the intimacy of being touched there, from the soft, slick stroke of his tongue over me in a place I'd barely touched myself. When he took a deep breath, as if smelling me, I squirmed. But when he sighed and laid his cheek on my hip, just staring at my bared pussy, my heart ached. A moment later, Sam was all business, and I came close to losing my mind.

I'd had an orgasm before. I think. I would have sworn I had before I learned what a real orgasm was from Sam. His mouth was just the beginning. He licked at me, tasting me, pushing his tongue deep inside where I was already wet and ready for him. When I couldn't stop squirming, he used his hands to hold me still, pulling back on my pussy to reveal my clit, swollen and flushed. His tongue stroking that little ball of nerves had my head rolling against the bed, keening whimpers coming from my open mouth.

I hadn't known anything could feel that good.

Hadn't imagined it. His lips locked onto my clit and sucked, then licked, then sucked again, working my pussy until I exploded in an orgasm that was unlike any pleasure I'd felt before.

Sam wasn't done after that. He waited, again resting his cheek on my hip as I shivered and panted for breath. He'd shrugged off his shirt at some point and the sight of his broad, muscled chest was enough to get me hot all over again. I'd seen Sam without a shirt once before, at a company party on Lake Mead, and the sight had branded itself on my mind.

Tanned skin, defined pecs, a six pack leading down into a chiseled V of muscle between his hips. Kneeling at the end of his bed as he was, I couldn't see more, but I wanted to, just as that day at the lake I'd longed to peel off his trunks and see what he looked like fully naked instead of just half. I was propping myself up on my elbows to get a better look when Sam's hand fell between my legs, one finger probing the entrance to my body.

The sensation of being stretched sent a tremor through me. I collapsed back into the mattress, opening my legs even wider, lifting my hips in unspoken invitation.

"Sam," I moaned, saying so much more in my head. *Please*, and *more*, and *I want it*. All that came out, after his name, was incoherent babbling.

"Shh, Chloe. It's okay."

He rubbed at my clit, sending more shivers

through my body as his finger worked its way deeper inside me, opening my body in a way it hadn't been in so long, and then not very well. I was just getting my bearings when a second finger joined the first, the two thrusting inside me, stretching as they teased my swollen flesh. My hips pressed into his hand, thrusting up, my body falling out of my control. I didn't know if I was supposed to stop, or if I could stop. I only knew I wanted more.

His mouth took me to the edge of orgasm again, sucking and licking at my clit as his fingers fucked in and out of me, my hips rocking hard, taking as much as he could give me with just his hand. His two fingers were bigger than anything I'd felt before, and I knew they weren't close to the size of his cock.

Just thinking the word cock, thinking about Sam's cock replacing his fingers, was enough to tip me over. Pleasure, sharp edged and white hot, ripped through me. I think I screamed. I know I called his name, chanting *Sam, Sam, Sam* as I fell off the edge of the world.

CHAPTER SIX
Chloe

When I came back to myself, I was laying on the bed beside a very naked Sam. His eyes studied my face, taking in every eyelash flicker and hitched breath. His mouth dropped to touch mine, his kiss slow and leisurely. I tasted myself on his lips and shuddered in remembered pleasure. He was so good, and I had no idea what I was doing.

But I was willing to learn. Feeling his lips moving with mine, I thought about what he'd done, about doing it myself. Just because I'd never taken a man in my mouth before didn't mean I couldn't do it now. Rolling back, I propped myself up on my arm and let my eyes slide down Sam's body, taking the time to appreciate every ridge and dip of his muscles. I knew there was a gym in the lower level of the house, as well as one in our office building, and he used both on a regular basis. It showed.

His body was a sculpture, sun kissed skin, a scattering of hair on his chest a shade darker than the hair on his head. That oh-so-sexy V at his hips, narrowing into the most amazing cock I'd ever seen. I hadn't seen that many. The boy I'd slept with in college. A few in movies and a porn I'd watched with giggling girlfriends years ago. None of them came close to Sam. My most fevered imaginings didn't come close to Sam. He was thick, wider around than I'd expected, even after feeling him through his jeans. And long.

As if appreciating my appraisal, Sam's cock flexed against his belly. Surprised, I looked up to catch his amused, aroused eyes. My hand reached down to stroke him, but he caught my arm to stop me.

"Sweet Chloe. I'm so close to the edge, if you touch me, I'll come."

"Really?" I whispered.

"Really," he said. He toyed with my fingers and said, "Are you done? We can wait for the rest and just go to sleep. It's late."

"No," I said before he'd finished. "No. Please, Sam. I swear, I'm ready. I want this. I want you."

"I want you too, love." He pulled me down for a kiss, whispering against my lips, "I feel like I've wanted you forever. Been dreaming of having you here forever. There hasn't been anyone else. Not for months."

"What?" I knew that couldn't be true. He'd been out with other women. I'd seen him in the paper, photographed with Dylan and Axel at various functions.

"I haven't slept with anyone for months, Chloe. Do you understand what I'm trying to say?"

"No," I answered truthfully. For the first time I was getting that I didn't understand anything.

"Are you on birth control?" he asked, seemingly changing the subject. I nodded, explaining, with a flush on my cheeks,

"I get bad cramps." My words trailed off. So silly. This man had his mouth between my legs and I was blushing over cramps. He didn't seem to care. Tucking my hair behind my ear, he said,

"I got tested at my check-up last month. I'm completely clean. I promise. But I'll get a condom if you want."

I thought about it for a second. That was all it took. I wouldn't get pregnant and I trusted that Sam wouldn't lie about being clean. I knew I was since, I been living like a nun.

"No, we don't need one. I want to feel all of you."

With a sound that was half groan and half laugh, Sam said, "You'll feel all of me love. You're so tight I'm going to hurt you if I'm not careful."

"Sam," I whispered, tired of waiting. "Please."

"Anything you want, Chloe."

Sam rose over me, fitting himself between my legs. Instinctively, I raised my knees and pulled my feet close to my hips, opening for him. When the head of his cock brushed my pussy, hot and hard, I jumped a little, too keyed up and aroused to stay still.

"Shhh," Sam whispered in my ear. "We're going slow. A little at a time."

He was true to his word. The head of his cock pressed inside me slowly, stretching me open, filling me so much more than his fingers had. I gasped and began to pant, willing my body to relax and make room for him. I couldn't think, couldn't put the feeling into words. It hurt. Not terribly, but the stretch and invasion weren't exactly comfortable. At the same time, it felt so good, as if all the empty places inside me were being broken open and remade the right way.

I lifted my knees and rolled my hips into his, taking another inch. Sam gasped and swore. "Fuck, Chloe. I'm trying to go slow here."

"I want more, Sam. Please," I panted. He was so gentle. So careful with me. And I knew he was right. I was tight. God, I could feel exactly how tight I was. Every tiny bit he moved deeper was a new pulling, stretching sensation. Sparks of pain and sharp, biting pleasure flickered back and forth, making me crazy.

Instead of moving my hips, I arched my back, raising my breasts to Sam. He was taller than me, but with only part of his cock inside me, he had plenty of room to dip his head and draw my nipple into his mouth.

I cried out at the liquid heat as he sucked. There was a line of nerves going straight from my nipple to my clit and with every draw of his mouth I felt the heat between my legs rise. My hips began to move again, out of my control, flexing and rolling, taking his cock in deeper, inch by inch. I cried out, the suck of his mouth and the invasion of his cock too much at once.

"Jesus, fuck, Chloe," Sam cried out as my pussy clamped down on his cock, my orgasm a wave of pleasure so big I was drowning in it. Sam finally lost control, slamming the rest of the way into me, fucking me hard, his cock remaking my pussy with every thrust, claiming me as his. I took it all, every flash of pain driving me higher. I don't know if I came more than once, or if I just came so long I blacked out.

The next thing I remember, I was laying on top of Sam, his still half-hard cock inside me, my head tucked beneath his chin, his hand stroking over my back and tangling in my hair.

"You okay?" he asked.

All I could say was, "Mmm." I trailed my fingers down his side, hardly able to believe I was lying naked in bed with Sam, his body still inside mine.

"Clo? Seriously, you okay?"

I shifted to raise my head so I could meet his eyes. "Seriously," I said. "I'm good. I'm amazing."

"Yes, you are," he said. I giggled, knowing he knew that wasn't what I'd meant.

The movement brushed my nipples against his chest hair, sparking a tiny burst of arousal. I squirmed, suddenly aware of Sam's cock inside me in a whole new way. The tingles between my legs increased as he hardened. With an incredulous laugh, Sam flipped me onto my back.

"I don't think I've rebounded that fast since I was a teenager," he said, dipping his head to nip the side of my neck. "So perfect, Chloe," he whispered in my ear. "Your pussy is perfect. I'm never letting you out of this bed."

"Fine with me," I whispered back, wrapping my legs around Sam's lean hips, taking all of his cock as he drove it deep. The stretch was less painful, more pressure than anything. The pleasure though that was even better.

This time we went slow, taking our time with long, drugging kisses, our hands roaming and stroking, bodies moving in sync, connected by more than the physical. I fell asleep in Sam's arms, feeling like I was exactly where I was meant to be.

CHAPTER SEVEN
Sam

"Where's Chloe?" Dad asked the second I walked into the kitchen.

"Sleeping," I said, not wanting to say more. If I had my way she'd sleep all day. We hadn't gotten back from the bar until well after midnight, and I'd kept her up until early morning making love to her. I hadn't had sex that many times in one night, ever. Not even when I was in college. But I'd finally had Chloe naked, and I hadn't been able to get enough of her. Now she needed her rest.

I had a meeting that afternoon I couldn't miss, but there was no reason she couldn't stay home and nap. I'd go to the meeting and get back as soon as I could. The company could run itself for one day without us. It would have to. Chloe was in my bed. I wasn't willing to let her out for at least a week. Maybe a month. Maybe I'd just have IT set up a laptop and she could work from my bedroom.

"What was going on last night?" Dad asked, interrupting my thoughts. "I heard you go out, then Chloe go out, and when you got back you were both yelling. What did you do?"

"I didn't do anything," I said, annoyed he assumed that I'd been the one who fucked up. My Dad and I got along great most of the time. He'd been my biggest supporter my entire life, and we rarely argued. Except over Chloe.

He'd been bugging me about Chloe since I'd hired her. First he was worried I'd get involved with her. My previous assistant had been about ninety and not a temptation in any way. When I'd hired Chloe, I hadn't seen her as one either. I'd noticed she had a pretty face and nice hair, but she'd dressed like a nun with no fashion sense and I'd had my head too far up my ass to notice how beautiful she was.

Then Dad had gotten to know Chloe better, and he'd been on my ass about *not* dating her. That had been worse. I couldn't go out with her, she was my assistant. And I dated plenty of women, why did he have to harp on about Chloe? But he insisted she was perfect for me. It got to the point where I forbade him to mention her name or scowl at me when I went out with another woman. Still, he wouldn't let it go, giving me looks all the time in the office when he caught us leaving together or eating lunch.

After the day we got caught in the rain and Chloe's wet dress opened my eyes, my Dad's nagging bugged me even more. By then I knew he was right, and I was pissed I couldn't do anything about it.

"You slept with her, didn't you?" he asked.

"Keep it down, Dad," I said. All I needed was Chloe to walk into the middle of my Dad telling me how to handle her.

"Don't fuck this up, Sammy. Of all the women you've brought home, she's the only one who counts."

"Leave it," I said, not wanting to talk about this with him. I knew she was the most important woman I'd ever been with. For fucks sake, I'd done everything I could to convince her of that. I didn't need my Dad, who hadn't had a serious girlfriend in over a decade, giving me romantic advice. I filled my favorite coffee cup with water and made myself some coffee, avoiding my Dad's eyes as I waited for the cup to fill.

"Sam, I'm not kidding. You need to lock her down. You never should have taken her to that pool hall. And what was she doing going out last night?"

"Dad, back off. I can't 'lock her down'." I made obnoxious air quotes as I repeated his phrase, my annoyance growing. *He* should fucking try to lock her down. See if she listened to him any better than she did to me.

At the memory of Dog's eyes on her, I felt sick. In the aftermath of finally making love to Chloe, I'd temporarily forgotten about the night before. Logic told me that if Nolan was in with Tsepov that deep,

Tsepov already had eyes on Chloe. But suspecting that and knowing she'd been in his territory were two different things. I could live with the first. I was finding it hard to accept the second.

"Well? Where did she go when she left?"

I sighed. "She followed me to the bar where Axel and I met our contact."

"Fucking A, Sam. You have to do a better job with her than this. She's going to get herself hurt."

"I know that, Dad," I said, making an attempt to keep my voice low but not succeeding. Taking a breath, I tried to calm down. "I know. But it isn't as simple as it seems. She's not going to sit back and let me do everything for her. And she's terrified for her brother."

"Should she be?" he asked, worry for Chloe distracting him from his mission to run my love life.

"Yeah. He's in a bad situation. Best case is that we find him and he gets Tsepov what he wants and he ends up alive and still working for Tsepov."

"That's your best case?"

"Yeah. I don't think Chloe realizes how bad it is. Not yet, anyway. She'll be crushed when she does."

"Is she in danger?" Dad's voice was heavy. He hadn't been giving me so much shit about Chloe just because he liked her for me. When it came down to it, my Dad liked her for her.

"She could be," I admitted.

"Then get her the fuck out of here, Sam. Let Axel

handle finding the brother and take Chloe away. Go on a vacation or something." I laughed.

"Sure, that would work. She's torn up over her missing brother, but she's going to hop on a plane and go on vacation with me. I can't keep her from chasing every lead we find. You think I can talk her into walking away?"

"Try harder then. Lie to her. Tell her whatever your have to. Convince her you're in love with her. Do whatever you have to to get her somewhere safe."

"Dad, back off. I'm not going to try to *convince* Chloe I'm in love with her. That's not what this is. Stop pushing so hard. We're fine without your help."

"Then find a way to stop her from going after Nolan."

"I'm trying, Dad. I'm doing everything I can to keep her from going out there and looking for Nolan."

"I'm just saying, if you put your mind to it, you could get her out of here," he said stubbornly.

"Yeah, you think it's so easy? You try it. I'd love to see how you do trying to pry her away from Vegas when her brother is missing and men with guns are looking for him. Good luck."

"You give her too much leeway," he grumbled.

"She's not a cocker spaniel, Dad. She's a woman who knows her own mind. Even if some of her decisions lately have been questionable. I agree, she's letting her loyalty to Nolan override her good sense.

But Chloe is smart. I respect her. And I'm not going to tell her I love her to get her to do something. How I feel about Chloe is between her and me. I'll tell her when it's the right time, not because I want to manage her."

My Dad shook his head. "You kids and your modern notions about equality. In my day, we told a woman what to do, and, and she did it."

"Yeah, right. Well, that explains why I'm the one who can get a woman to say yes to a second date."

"Just watch out for her, Sam," he said, all the sarcasm gone from his voice. "We can't let anything happen to her."

"I know Dad. I know."

My Dad left the kitchen and headed for the garage, by then a few minutes late to get to his site on time. I thought about waking Chloe, but knew I wouldn't. She needed her sleep. I had a pile of email on my laptop and most likely a few fires to put out, especially since Chloe was sleeping instead of managing things in the office.

Grabbing my coffee, I decided to get a little work done before Chloe woke up.

CHAPTER EIGHT
Chloe

I stood in the hall, my knees shaking as I listened to Sam tell his Dad to back off. I didn't usually eavesdrop. I'd learned the hard way after listening to a friend talk about me in high-school that eavesdroppers rarely hear what they want to.

Normally I would have walked right into the kitchen. It wasn't the first time I'd refereed a disagreement between Sam and his dad. But something in the hushed yet angry tone of their voices held me back. I couldn't hear anything clearly until Sam said, *Dad, back off. I'm not going to try to convince Chloe I'm in love with her. That's not what this is. Stop pushing so hard. We're fine without your help.* Then, *I'm doing everything I can to keep her from going out there and looking for Nolan.*

My knees went weak, and I backed down the hall, not wanting to be seen. Daniel's response was drowned out by the rush of blood in my ears as I crept back to Sam's bedroom. Moving on auto-pilot, I went straight to the bathroom and turned on the shower, getting beneath the spray before it warmed up. I didn't notice the cold. Sam's words had filled me with ice.

I'm not going to try to convince Chloe I'm in love with her. That's not what this is.

That's not what this is.

No, of course it wasn't. We'd had sex. A lot of sex. I'd fallen asleep dreaming of love and he was just glad we'd finally fucked. He'd said he wanted me. He'd said he cared for me. But he never said he loved me. He never promised that this was more than sex. He said he didn't want an affair, and stupidly, I'd assumed that meant he wanted more.

My chest felt like it had been caved in, hollow and bleeding. I sank to the floor of the shower, letting the water beat down on my head, and cried. I'd known getting involved with Sam would break my heart. I just hadn't realized it would happen this fast.

It felt like hours later when I finally ran out of tears. Moving out of habit, I washed my hair and my body, then stepped out of the shower to brush my teeth and blow my hair dry. I couldn't do anything about Sam. I'd been foolish in sleeping with him. But I knew that before I did it. Now that was over, but I had a job to do, and Nolan was still missing.

I didn't want to talk to Sam about what I'd overheard. It seemed clear enough. And I didn't think I could handle any more humiliation. Besides, there was that other part I'd overheard.

I'm doing everything I can to keep her from going out there and looking for Nolan.

I knew he didn't think it was safe for me to try to find my brother. And he had a point. I was out of my depth dealing with stolen information and Russian mobsters. But I hadn't realized he was actively trying to stop me. It hadn't felt like that. His words gave him away. If I wanted to get out of this situation with my dignity intact, if not my heart, I was going to have to be clever.

We had a meeting that afternoon, rather *Sam* had a meeting. One he couldn't miss. It was out of the office and he'd be gone for at least three hours. If I could convince him that everything was business as usual, it would give me the perfect chance to leave without an argument.

I was being a coward. But I was okay with that. I've been more open with Sam, more vulnerable, than I'd been with any other human being in my entire life. I couldn't go there again, couldn't open myself up to talk about the things he'd said, couldn't leave myself raw and exposed only to feel more pain. I had to pull myself together and move on. Had to focus on what was really important. My family. Nolan.

Standing in front of my new clothes hanging in Sam's closet, I considered the problem of getting away. I couldn't go back to my apartment. And most of my clothes there were ruined anyway. But Sam's meeting should give me plenty of time to get back here, pack a bag, and find somewhere else to stay. I didn't have a lot in my savings account, but it was enough to cover a hotel for a week or so until I found Nolan. Then maybe it was time the Henson family considered relocating.

At the thought of leaving Las Vegas, of leaving Sam, my heart squeezed in my chest and tears sprang to my eyes. For a second I ran over in my head everything I'd heard Sam say, hoping there was another interpretation. Maybe I just hadn't stayed long enough. Maybe he'd said something else. I caught sight of my face in a mirror and the image of my puffy red eyes hit me like a slap. I was being sad and desperate. I loved him, and he'd said "That's not what this is." And then he'd admitted he was actively trying to stop me from finding Nolan.

Well, fine then. I'd made a mistake, but it wasn't the end of the world. I certainly wasn't the first woman to sleep with her boss and regret it later. Choosing a charcoal gray suit from the closet, I pulled on the plum colored shell Lola had hung with it and slid my feet into the matching plum heels. It was probably wrong to take the clothes with me. At that moment I didn't care.

I was feeling more than a little beat up, and every woman knows a brand-new wardrobe is a pretty good band-aid for a broken heart. So was ice cream, but the last thing I needed was another few inches on my hips.

Dressed and makeup done, I took a deep breath for strength and left the bedroom. I didn't want coffee, or breakfast. We'd only put in a half day at the office the day before and my desk was probably piled high. Never mind that I wasn't even sure if I'd be going back after today. If I wanted my plan to work, Sam had to think everything was business as usual.

I found him at the dining room table, his laptop and papers spread out around him, his eyes locked on to the view of Vegas sprawling outside the window. When he heard the sound of my heels clicking on the hardwood he turned and smiled, a smile so sweet and happy I wanted to cry. He pushed back from the table and came towards me, hands outstretched.

"What are you doing up?" he asked. "You need to rest. You haven't been getting much sleep lately, and I kept you up late last night. I thought you could take the day off."

"You have that meeting in Henderson at one," I said, stepping to the side to evade his outstretched hands. I didn't want to kiss him, but I wasn't sure how to avoid it without raising questions I wasn't strong enough to answer. Sam stepped back, his hands dropping, eyes confused.

"I can handle that without you," he said. "Why

don't you just stay here and relax?"

Stalling for time to think, I went into the kitchen to make myself a cup of coffee. I was already dressed for work, but I could change into something else. And it would be easier to leave from here. I went back into the dining room with my coffee and sat in one of the chairs at the table across from Sam, preventing him from coming any closer.

He studied me, his expression cautious. He knew something was up. I've never been able to lie to him very well, not that I tried that often. I wasn't a liar by nature. But every once in a while, when he asked a question I didn't want to answer, like 'who ate the last chocolate chip cookie?', I'd fib. He always caught me.

"Are you sure?" I asked. I really did have a lot to get done in the office. I wasn't sure how everything was going to work out with Sam long-term, but it wasn't fair to anyone for me to blow off my job because my affair with the boss hadn't gone as planned.

"I'm sure," he said. "Stay home. Axle's working on finding Nolan. You can take the day off, rest, I'll leave my laptop so you can check email and deal with anything that's really pressing."

"Okay, if you're sure." This was so weird. Only a few hours ago I'd been ready to give Sam everything, now it was all I could do to keep myself from running out of the room.

"Clo, are you okay?" Sam asked, his blue eyes sharp as they fixed on my face. "You're acting weird."

"I'm not," I said. "I'm acting normal in a weird situation."

"You're being a goof. This isn't a weird situation, it's just different. You'll get used to it and it'll seem like it was always this way."

His words felt like a punch to my stomach. I couldn't reconcile the way he was being with the things he'd said to Daniel. He was acting like everything was fine. Like we were together. Maybe I'd misunderstood. Maybe I'd misheard and jumped to conclusions. Maybe I just needed to woman up and ask Sam what was going on.

Putting my coffee mug down on the table, I sucked in a quick breath and said, "Sam? What is it that I'm going to get used to?" He gave me a look as if I was a little slow.

"This. Us. You and me being together."

"Are we? Together?"

Sam studied me, silent, his thoughts hidden behind suddenly blank eyes. "Chloe, so much is going on right now. Can we just be how we are for a while before we talk about it?"

An answer that was no answer at all. My heart sank. It wasn't, "Of course we're together, Chloe. What did you think last night was?" It definitely wasn't, "Of course we're together, I love you Chloe, and I always will."

I wondered how many other women had sat at

his table and gotten some version of the "let's just be how we are" speech. A lot. And I was the next one on the list. Pulling together every one of my feeble skills in deception, I manufactured a placid smile for Sam and said, "Sure. We'll talk about it later."

I looked at the time and was relieved to see it was after eleven. I'd spent way longer getting ready than I normally did. I must've been in the shower for over forty-five minutes.

"You're going to have to leave soon, unless you brought the specs for the meeting home with you yesterday," I said, knowing he hadn't.

"Shit, I didn't. I thought we'd go into the office this morning."

"If you leave now, you'll have time to review everything before you have to go."

I picked up my coffee and drank. From the hesitant look on Sam's face I could tell that he wasn't entirely buying it. Either he suspected I was trying to get rid of him, or he knew I was up to something. At the very least he could tell I wasn't being straight with him. I thought about making an excuse to go change, since I didn't need to wear a suit today if I wasn't going into work, but that might give Sam the idea to join me in the bedroom. If he touched me, I would break.

"Do you mind if I make myself something to eat?" I asked.

"Anything you want, Clo. Make yourself at home.

I'll be back as soon as I can." Sam got up from the table and began stacking the papers in front of him. I stayed where I was, but said,

"Go change. I'll get your briefcase packed."

"Thanks, honey."

Sam left, pausing only briefly to kiss the top of my head. I felt the touch of his lips all the way down my spinal cord. I was desperately glad that as he walked away he couldn't see my tears.

CHAPTER NINE
Chloe

I thought he would never leave. I'd wiped my eyes and gotten to work sorting and organizing the papers spread across the dining room table, putting them back in his briefcase so he'd be able to find everything easily when he needed it. By the time he came back, wearing a deep navy suit with a blue shirt and crisply striped tie, I was ready to lose it.

I'd always loved the way Sam looked in a suit. He wasn't one of those uber-polished men, with perfect hair and buffed nails who looked like they could be a menswear model. Sam was too masculine for that. His blond hair a little too thick and unruly, his jaw a little too square, and his shoulders too broad.

He looked most at home in a pair of tough khaki work pants and construction boots, out on the site with one of his crews. But when you put him in a suit, it always seemed to me like trying to restrain something primal. And now that I knew what he looked like without anything on it all, my fingers itched to loosen his tie and yank it off.

Too bad my heartbreak couldn't seem to get the message through to my hormones. I ate him up with my eyes while my brain warned me to stay away. I would. I was leaving. But I had a hard time letting him go. I handed him his briefcase and assured him I'd be fine on my own.

When he was gone, I went back to the bedroom to change out of my suit. I wasn't going to rush, just in case Sam forgot something and came back. Standing in the closet, I hung the suit and plum shell back on the hanger the way Lola had arranged them. I didn't have a suitcase, but fortunately most of what Lola sent over had come in department store garment bags. My conscience chirped at me, telling me I should leave the clothes. I ignored it. Leaving the clothes would be stupid. Sam couldn't use them. He'd bought them for me.

He was going to be angry I'd left, there was no question about that. But he'd probably be even more pissed if I left the things he'd bought me. At least, that was what I told myself. Trying to think ahead, I borrowed a small gym bag from the back of Sam's closet, one I recognized as a vendor giveaway we'd all gotten the year before. I packed it with enough clothes to hold me for the next few days. None of the suits or dresses, just casual wear and a few pairs of shoes.

The rest of the clothes I replaced in the garment bags and carried out to my car, laying them neatly down in the trunk where they wouldn't get wrinkled or damaged. I checked the clock. Just after noon. There was no way Sam would be back before his one o'clock meeting. He wouldn't have time.

While I'd been packing I'd worked out a rough plan. I'd stay in a hotel on the other side of town, someplace off the strip which was the last place Sam would expect me to be. Then, I'd call Tim and see if I could get him to meet me. He'd known about Dog and the poker room. He must know more even if he didn't think he did. I just had to find out what it was.

I almost used Sam's laptop to book a hotel room, then thought better of it and did it on my phone. I chose one that was low-profile but not run down. Something with a bar and a restaurant, not right on the strip but close enough that it would be crowded. I wasn't exactly experienced at hiding in plain sight, but it seemed logical that the bigger the crowd, the more I'd blend in.

I changed into a casual sky blue shirt-dress. It was similar to some of the dresses I used to wear to work, except cut much better. My old dresses were boxy, the shoulders padded, hiding my breasts and hips. This one was trim through the shoulders, with cute cap sleeves, a flared skirt, and a wide belt that made my waist look smaller. There was nothing provocative about it. As dresses went it was fairly demure.

But with my very curvy figure, it was still a bit sexy. I buttoned up one more button on the bodice to make sure there was no hint of cleavage and slipped into a pair of matching flat sandals. In this I looked like any other tourist.

I felt like a criminal as I backed my car out of the garage and drove through the gates at the end of Sam's driveway. Whatever was going on between us, I absolutely knew he didn't want me to leave. He'd be furious when he found out I had. I didn't see another choice. I needed to find Nolan, and Sam had admitted to Daniel that he was doing everything he could to stop me. I couldn't live with that.

With everything I'd learned in the past few days about my brother, I was growing more and more aware that he was in deep shit. So deep, I doubted I could save him. I had to try. No matter how much of a mess Nolan might be, I would never turn my back on my brother. Never. And Sam was wrong to try to make me.

I drove to the hotel on autopilot, running through different scenarios in my mind. Was Nolan really hiding? Or was he out there somewhere fucking around and playing cards? Maybe I could get Tim to tell me some of the other places Nolan played and go look there.

Checking in was quick. The hotel didn't have valet, which was easier, and I was parked and done with the front desk ten minutes after I got there. The room was nothing to get excited about. It was clean, and the hallway was quiet. That was all I cared about.

Fatigue dragged at me. Sam had been right, I hadn't been sleeping well and the few hours I got in the night before weren't nearly enough. I stared at the bed and thought about laying down, just for a few minutes. Not a good idea. I needed to keep moving. Needed to talk to Tim.

I called him from my cell and was relieved when he picked up on the second ring saying, "Nolan?"

"No, Tim. It's me, Chloe."

"Oh, sorry. I guess I was hoping it was Nolan again," He said, sheepishly.

"So you haven't heard from him?"

"No, I would've called if I had."

"Listen, Tim, do you think you could meet me? I just want to ask you some questions about Nolan. I've learned some new things and I'm just wondering if maybe you know things you don't know you know. If that makes sense."

"Um, kind of? It kind of makes sense. What did you find out?"

"I don't want to talk about it over the phone," I said. "Could you meet me for coffee or a drink or something? I haven't had lunch yet."

"Sure I could meet you for lunch," Tim said easily.

"Great." The restaurant at the hotel looked good enough. I told him where I was staying and he agreed to meet me there in half an hour. I killed time by checking email on my phone, handling a few things that had popped up at work and watching the clock as the minutes ticked by.

Tim was waiting for me outside the restaurant when I got there. Unlike the day before, he didn't look like he'd picked his clothes up off the floor. He wore clean jeans, white sneakers, and a gray zip up hoodie with the company logo on the left side. His hair was clean and brushed, his eyes bright but clear. Too late, I remembered what Sam had said about him acting like a tweaker, but he seemed completely sober, to my relief.

"I'm starved," he said when I walked up. "I was at work late last night finishing up a project and I missed dinner. Feels like I've been living off vending machine junk for the last week."

"I'm hungry, too," I said, leading the way into the restaurant. I glanced at the menu, not really caring what I got, and ordered a ruben when the waitress came by. Tim ordered more food than I could imagine he could stuff in his skinny body. A double cheeseburger, onion rings, and a milkshake. More worried about Nolan than food, I leaned forward and said in a low voice,

"Did you know Nolan was working for Tsepov?" I asked. Tim's eyes widened almost comically, and he looked around as if to assure himself no one was listening.

"Where did you hear that?"

"From a guy named Feliks at a pool hall," I said watching Tim carefully. His shock seemed genuine, but was he surprised to hear what Nolan was doing? Or surprised that I knew? It was impossible to say.

"No, I didn't know. I knew he got into Tsepov for some money. I'm sorry I didn't tell you that yesterday but I didn't want to freak you out."

"It's okay," I said. I was lying, but so was Tim. I could see it on his face. He'd known Nolan was in with Tsepov over more than money lost in a poker game.

"He'll turn up, Chloe. I'm sure he will."

"I can't stop looking, Tim. He's my brother. What if he needs my help?"

"I'm not trying to scare you, Chloe. But if he's running from Tsepov, he needs more help than you can give him."

The waitress came and dropped our food between us. Tim grabbed an onion ring the second the plate hit the table and shoved it in his mouth. Not waiting to finish chewing before he spoke, he said "What happened to the guy who was with you yesterday?"

Something about the way he looked at me when he asked struck me as odd. I wasn't going to share my personal issues with Tim, who wasn't exactly a friend. Again, I lied, kind of.

"He has a meeting right now, otherwise he'd be with me. Can you think of any places Nolan might be hiding out? Any friends he might be with? Is it possible he's just out on a bender or playing cards?"

"I don't know Chloe. I really doubt he's out there partying."

"But why? How do you know he's in trouble? Maybe he paid Tsepov the money he owed him and he's just messing around."

"I don't, I guess. I mean, I got the impression he was in trouble from you."

Had he? That didn't make sense if he knew Nolan owed Tsepov money. I'd only just learned who most of the players were in this situation, but even I knew owing a Russian mobster money put you right in the middle of a lot of trouble. I couldn't put my finger on it, but something about Tim felt off.

Making me even more uneasy, he reached out and took my hand in his. Meeting my eyes, his own insistently sincere, he said, "Chloe, don't worry about Nolan. I'm sure he'll be fine."

As gently as I could, I took my hand back, saying "I can't help it, Tim. He's my brother. Please, if you can think of anywhere he might be, will you tell me?"

"Let me think about it," Tim said, picking up his burger and taking a huge bite.

I tried not to sigh in annoyance. Clearly, the conversation was on hold until Tim had filled his stomach. I was hungry too, so I went ahead and ate my reuben while Tim inhaled his significantly larger meal. He was done in record time. It was shocking, to be honest, how quickly such as skinny guy could eat that much food.

When he had sucked down the last dregs of his milkshake, Tim sat back and folded his hands over his stomach.

"I can take a long lunch today," he said. "I've been working late every night this week, so they'll cut me some slack. I really don't know where Nolan is, but I can take you around to a few of the places we play cards and see if anybody's heard from him."

Relief washed through me. I wasn't wild about going off with Tim, especially after he'd grabbed my hand like that. We didn't know each other well enough to be holding hands. But this felt like progress. At least with Tim I'd be out there, talking to people who knew Nolan.

Maybe we'd get lucky. With every hour that went by I was more scared for my brother. I was willing to admit he was kind of a fuck-up, but he was mine. I'd raised him. I loved him. I'd do anything I had to to get him back.

CHAPTER TEN
Chloe

I shouldn't have been surprised when Tim let me pay for lunch. It was only fair; I guess. I had invited him. We left the restaurant and went out of the hotel by a side door, headed for the parking garage and my car. Tim was on the phone with someone, checking around to see if anybody had seen Nolan more recently than Saturday. It didn't sound like he was having any luck.

I was so focused on listening to Tim's conversation; I wasn't paying attention to our surroundings. The parking garage was above ground, but I had parked on the first level so it was a little dim out of the bright afternoon sunshine. Maybe that was why I didn't notice the shadowy figures closing in on us from both sides. I wouldn't have seen them at all if I hadn't spun around at the last second, worried I'd led us past my car.

By the time I registered what was happening, it

was too late. I saw Tim hit the ground, his phone spinning out of his hand when he hit the pavement. I was lifted up and back, my arms wrenched behind me and secured with the click of handcuffs. I tried to turn my head and see who had me, but all I got was a glimpse of dark hair before a black bag fell over my head. I was lifted and dropped into a stiff seat, something tight drawn across my chest and fastened with a click. A seatbelt?

Doors slammed, an engine started, and I swayed in the seat as we took off out of the parking garage. I fought against my rising panic. As much as I tried to get myself under control, I might've really lost it if the black bag hadn't been whipped off my head, leaving me staring at a familiar face. A very angry familiar face.

Axel.

"Let me go," I said. "What the hell are you doing? You can't kidnap me."

Axel laughed. "I just did," he said. "And you're not going anywhere until Sam gets here. And then only if he agrees to keep a handle on you."

Infuriated, I jerked against the handcuffs and pulled on the seatbelt. I was strapped into a narrow seat in the back of a cargo van. Axel sat on a similar seat, facing me. "Let me go," I said, my angry voice filling the van. "This is ridiculous. You can't do this."

All the humor was wiped from Axel's face. "You know what's ridiculous? You, wondering around Las

Vegas, trying to hook up with the Russian mob to help your fuck-up of a brother. That's what's fucking ridiculous. I get loyalty, Chloe. I respect it. You're a good woman. And I know you're smart. Except when it comes to your brother. Sam's told you, Daniel's told you, and I'm telling you again – keep your fucking head down and let me and my guys do our jobs. If Nolan can be found, we'll find him. Right now, the good news is that no one knows where he is. It seems like he can do one thing right, and that's hide like a weasel."

"Hey! Stop talking about him like that," I protested. Evidence was showing that Nolan was a fuck-up and possibly also a weasel. But he was my brother, and only I could call him those things.

"I'll say whatever the fuck I want about a guy who would get wrapped up with the mob and put the sister who's given him everything in danger. You deserve better than this, Chloe. And as much as I respect your loyalty, he's shitting all over it."

"That's for me to decide, isn't it?" I asked, quietly.

"Normally, yeah," Axel said. "Not this time. You don't seem to understand that you're putting your life in danger. Or maybe you understand and you don't care. I thought you were smarter than that."

"I can't just sit at home and wait."

"I get that, Chloe. I know what you do every day. I know you're the woman that makes things happen for Sam, that you spend all your time ensuring that everything around you works the way it should for everyone you care about. And I know it goes against the grain to sit back and trust that other people are doing it for you. But you are not qualified to deal with this shit. And no one, not Sam, not me, no one, wants you anywhere near these people. Last night was a clusterfuck of epic proportions. Did you know my guy wasn't the only one watching you today?"

"You've been watching me?"

Axel shook his head at my naiveté, laughing at me again. "Yeah, most of my guys on your case are looking for Nolan, but ever since Sam found you in the model home, I've had a guy on you at all times. How do you think we found you so fast?"

"I hadn't thought about that yet," I said.

When I was planning my grand escape it had never occurred to me that I was under surveillance. I really was a disaster at all of this cloak and dagger stuff. It was a good thing I was an executive assistant at a development company and I didn't work for Axel.

"What do you mean your guy wasn't the only guy watching me today?" I asked, fear collecting in a leaden ball in my stomach.

"I haven't had a chance to tell Sam yet, he's been in a meeting all afternoon. But there was another guy watching you today. We think he works for Tsepov, but we're not positive yet. We're still working on it."

"Who else could it be?"

"There are some players in this we haven't identified yet," Axel said, stretching his legs out in front of him and crossing his arms over his chest. He seemed completely at ease on the uncomfortable narrow seat in the back of the van. "We know that Nolan got the information Tsepov wanted. We know he never gave the information to Tsepov. There seems to be speculation as to whether he plans to sell the information to another party, or whether he can't get close enough to make the delivery without being intercepted."

"What is it that he has?" I asked.

"I don't know," Axel said, grimly. "And I don't want to know. You don't want to know. Whatever Nolan has is important to a lot of people. We've gotten some hints that some of the parties after it are working for Tsepov and involved in their own double-cross. They may be using Nolan as a scapegoat. It would explain why he's having such a hard time making the delivery."

"How do you know he's not double-crossing Tsepov?" I asked, the words sticking in my throat.

"I don't, yet. It's just a hunch. But when we talk to people, most of them are sure Nolan wouldn't try to fuck with Tsepov. And the few people who suggested it are suspicious enough on their own to make me think they have their own agenda."

"So why aren't you following them? Why aren't you-"

"Chloe, enough. I know my job. And you know that I know my job. Let. Me. Do. It. Stop getting in my way. Go home to Sam, work from the house for a few days and let us find your brother. Can you do that?"

"No." I wished I could cross my arms over my chest in a mockery of Axle's position. I also wished my glare was half as good as his. I wasn't intimidating enough, and Axle could be scary when he was smiling.

"Why the fuck not?" Axel asked, exasperated.

"I'm not going back to Sam," I said and looked away, not wanting Axel to see the pain on my face.

"I thought you two finally worked things out."

"What does that mean?" I asked.

"You know what it means. You two have been hot for each other for so long it's a miracle you manage to get any work done. Then he drags you out of the bar last night, and I know you went home and fought, because you were pissed, too. Don't tell me you didn't end up in bed."

I looked away and pressed my lips together, willing the tears back from my eyes. I refused to cry in front of Axel. He was a rock, and I didn't want him to see my weakness. Worse, what if he told Sam I was crying over him? I didn't think I could bear that.

"He fucked it up, didn't he?" Axel asked, shaking his head. "Un-fucking believable. The guy can get any woman with no effort. He has the only one he really wants right in front of him all day, every day, and he still manages to fuck it up."

"I don't think you understand," I said, with as much dignity as I could muster. "Sam and I made a mistake, that's all."

"No, Chloe, I don't think *you* understand."

"Axel," I snapped, tired of talking about this with him. "I heard him tell Daniel that he was only with me to keep me from looking for Nolan and that whatever was between us it wasn't something serious. I think that's pretty plain. And it's none of your business so can we please stop talking about Sam?"

"I don't suppose you'd trust me if I told you that there is no way Sam meant that."

I shook my head. "No, I don't trust you. I know how close you are to Sam, and I know you'd probably lie if you thought it would get him out of trouble."

Axle laughed again. I was getting tired of his amusement at my expense. "I probably would. Forget that, I *have* lied to get him out of trouble. But I'm not lying now Chloe, I promise. It goes against the guy code to tell you this, but you're having a shit week, so I'm going to cut you a break."

"What?" I said, not wanting to hear whatever crap was going to come out of Axel's mouth.

He leaned forward, bracing his elbows on his knees, his body swaying in perfect balance with the van as it turned the corner. Axel wasn't my type, too hard-edged and intense. Besides, unfortunately for me, Sam had always been the only man I really wanted. But the part of me that wasn't stuck in a total emotional upheaval could appreciate that Axel was a very good-looking guy. Especially like this, his face soft, his eyes concerned but serious.

"Chloe," he said. "Sam has been crazy in love with you for longer than even he knows. And he's known how he's felt for months. He's so tied up in knots over you, he's been terrified to make a move, scared he'll drive you away and lose you. If he had any idea that some comment he made to Daniel had done exactly that, he'd be sick over it. Give him another chance. He's a good man, and he loves you."

Axle was so sincere I couldn't keep his words out of my heart. To my embarrassment, I burst into tears sobbing out, "He told Daniel he wouldn't tell me he loved me, that it wasn't what our relationship was about."

I heard Axel say, "Fuck," under his breath as he got off his seat and came towards me. Gently, more gently than I would've suspected Axel could, he wiped the tears off my face and took my chin in his hand, forcing me to meet his dark eyes.

"I don't know why he said that, Chloe. But I do know it's not true. And so do you. You know Sam," he said, wiping the tears from my cheeks again. "I know everything going on has you totally spun, and I know you're terrified for your brother, but you need to think. You know Sam, and you know he would never treat you like that."

I closed my eyes and looked away, afraid to believe Axel. I wanted to. I wanted it with everything I had. But it seemed like too much to hope for. All I've ever wanted in life was a family. I tried to make one with Nolan after our mom left and our dad started ignoring us. That hadn't worked out very well.

When I fell in love with Sam, impossibly and completely in love with a man I was sure would never love me back, it seemed like that dream was even further away. I wanted Sam to love me, so much that I couldn't bring myself to trust it.

Unable to get away from Axel and his eyes that saw everything, I squeezed mine shut. "Just go away," I whispered, pleading when I wanted to shout. "Please, Axel, please just leave me alone."

"Okay, sweetheart. When we get to my office, I'm taking the cuffs off and I'm locking you in our safe room until Sam gets there. Then I'll let you two work it out."

There was nothing to work out, but Axel would see that soon enough. I was too heartsick to care about convincing him.

CHAPTER ELEVEN
Sam

The meeting didn't go too badly considering I had my mind on Chloe half the time. Fortunately, it wasn't a complicated deal. A local construction firm had gone bankrupt, and the investors in one of their commercial developments were looking for someone to pick up the project. I had a crew just the right size wrapping up a project by the end of the month. They were ahead of schedule, so I could split the crew and get started on the new job right away.

Chloe would be happy. She'd hated the company who had the project before. The owner had been an obnoxious blow-hard who had some very outdated ideas about women. She hadn't been glad when his company went under, but she'd love that we'd picked up the job they'd lost.

Chloe. Something wasn't right with her. She'd been distant that morning, not meeting my eyes, in too much of a hurry to get me out of the house. I'd expected her to be skittish. She'd been so against us having a relationship and then she'd changed her mind so suddenly. I'd figured she'd back-peddle on me. Then why did I feel so uneasy? Axel had a guy on the house, so I knew she was safe. I hadn't set the alarm when I left; it was way too complicated to show her one time and hope she'd be able to operate it without setting it off. And I didn't want her to feel trapped.

By the time we'd all shook hands and left the conference room, it was pushing five o'clock. I'd left my phone in the truck, and I walked out eager to turn it back on and check on Chloe. I wasn't expecting to see multiple texts from Axel on top of three voicemails. All telling me to call him the second I was free. My gut tight with dread, I dialed his cell.

"Where the fuck have you been?" he asked, sounding pissed.

"In a meeting, exactly where I told you I'd be. What's wrong?"

"Chloe is a huge pain in my ass, that's what's wrong. You need to get in here and deal with your woman."

"Here where? Your office?"

"Yeah. My safe room, to be exact. I've had her locked in since I caught her meeting that tweaker friend of Nolan's off the strip a few hours ago."

"Fuck," I said. I didn't want her anywhere near that guy. "Is she okay?"

"She's pissed as hell. And she thinks you're just using her for sex."

"WHAT?!" I couldn't help yelling into the phone.

"Yeah, she overheard some conversation you had with Daniel and now she thinks you're using her for sex and your going to get rid of her as soon as she's not convenient. And she knows that you're trying to stop her from finding her brother. So she's pissed and miserable, which means I have a crying woman locked in my safe room. My safe room isn't for crying women, Sam. It's for locking down badasses and imprisoning guys we need to question. I don't even have tissues in there. Get your ass here and take her home where she belongs."

"I'm on my way. Is she okay? Physically okay? She didn't get hurt when she was with Tim?"

"Like I'd let anything happen to Chloe," Axel said. "She's fine, just extremely stressed out and unhappy."

I hung up on Axel and concentrated on getting downtown to his offices as fast as I could. *Fuck. Fuck. Fuck.* If Chloe had overheard my conversation with my dad that would explain a lot. I'd given dad the impression that things weren't that serious, or at least I tried to, but only to get my dad off my back. I should've just told him to butt out. Fuck. I was trying to figure out what to do when my phone rang. I looked down to see it was Dylan. A good friend of mine and Axel's, Dylan ran the Delecta casino. I'd invited him over for dinner a few days ago, along with his girlfriend Leigha.

I answered, trying to decide if dinner was still a good idea. At the time, Chloe hadn't been living with me. Would she want us to be alone, or would a distraction be better? My gut said distraction was the way to go. Chloe was far too polite to be rude to me in front of guests. And Dylan and Leigha had only been dating for a few weeks. They were still in that disgusting lovey-dovey phase where their hands were all over each other and they got caught staring into one another's eyes. It could be annoying, but it might also be a good influence on Chloe. I took the call, saying,

"Hey man, what's up?"

"We still on for dinner?" Dylan asked.

"Yeah, definitely. But I need a huge favor. Chloe's staying with me. She's having a bad time, her brother's missing - it's a long story."

"That sucks. Chloe's a sweetheart. Is Axel on it?"

"Yeah. And get this – the brother's tied up with Tsepov."

"Not good," Dylan said. He would know. Leigha had been attacked the month before by her ex-boyfriend who, like Nolan, had a gambling debt with Tsepov. Tsepov had taken the ex when he got out on bail after his attack on Leigha, and no one had seen him since.

"I know. And she's royally pissed at me for trying to keep her from finding her brother. Right now it's a mess."

"Are you sure you want to do dinner, then?"

"I don't think she's looking forward to spending the evening alone with me. Some company would be good. But can we do it at my place? I want Chloe somewhere secure. And would you mind bringing dinner with you? I've got the wine covered."

"No problem," Dylan said. "You have anything in mind, or should I pick?"

"It's up to you, whatever you guys want will be great."

"See you in an hour or two then." Dylan hung up, and I tossed my phone on the seat beside me.

Of the three of us, myself, Axel, and Dylan, Dylan had the best game with women. If anyone would know exactly what to bring for dinner with a stressed out, exhausted, emotional woman, it would be Dylan. And Leigha joining him was just a bonus. She was a perfect match for him, strong, funny, and absolutely gorgeous. She was also kind and friendly. I knew she'd make friends with Chloe right away. Which could backfire if they decided to gang up on me as the asshole guy making Chloe miserable. I was willing to take the risk.

I pulled into the parking garage beneath Axel's building, my mind racing. I had no idea what I was going to say to Chloe. And I couldn't begin to guess what she was planning to say to me. Getting out of the car, I realized I was just going to have to play it by ear. I'd fucked up today by trying to mislead my dad. And I'd lost all these months with Chloe by being too afraid to tell her how I felt.

Axel met me at the door and walked me back to their safe room, down several winding corridors and behind three separate security doors. As a rule, I didn't ask Axel details about his clients. I'd been in his offices a few times and they always reminded me that whatever Axel did, it wasn't simple security.

At the door to the safe room, Axel paused before punching in the code. Looking at me, he said, "Go easy with her, okay? I think she's at the end of her rope."

"I plan on it. Give me a minute, will you?"

He punched the code and swung the door open. "I'll turn off the cameras. Knock on the door when you're ready to come out."

I walked in to find Chloe fast asleep on the double bed in the corner, curled on her side, her hands stacked beneath her cheek, trails of tears staining her skin. My gut clenched. I'd done this to her. Not entirely, maybe. Some of it was her idiot brother. But my careless words had hurt her. It was the last thing I'd ever want to do.

Moving on instinct alone, I toed off my shoes and climbed into the bed beside her. Fitting my chest to her back like a spoon, I tucked my arm around her waist and held her, waiting for her to wake up. It was a testament to how exhausted she was that it took her more than five minutes to realize she was no longer alone. And despite what her head was telling her, her body still trusted me, because she woke slowly, her eyes fluttering open, her limbs relaxed. In a whisper she said,

"Sam?" Her voice was heavy with sleep.

"Right here, honey. Everything's okay."

In a flat tone that tore at me, she said, "Nothing's okay."

I lifted my hand to smooth her hair away from her face once, then again, unable to stop touching her soft, smooth cheeks. "It will be," I said. "I promise Chloe, it will be."

On a sob, Chloe said, "Sam. Sam, I can't-"

"Shhh, love. Shhh." I didn't know what else to do. She wept quietly, every hitching breath making me more desperate to fix what was wrong. I rolled her into me, pulling one thigh over my legs and tucking her face into my collarbone.

"Chloe," I said. "Chloe, love, don't cry. Don't cry." I buried one hand in her hair and rubbed the back of her head, hating how tight the muscles in her neck were. She was under too much stress and the pressure was breaking her. Not sure if it was the right thing to say, I forged ahead anyway and said,

"I'm sorry about this morning. What you heard me say to Daniel... I was lying because he was pissing me off. It's true, I've been trying to keep you from putting yourself into danger while you're looking for Nolan. I'm not going to apologize for that."

"Sam-"

"No, let me finish," I said. She raised her face to meet my eyes, hers tear drenched and painfully uncertain. "I won't use how I feel to manipulate you. That's not what this is between us. It's more. And this isn't how I wanted to tell you, but I need you to know. I love you. It feels like I've loved you forever."

My body was relaxed against Chloe's but inside I felt strung tight with apprehension. What if I'd misread everything? What if she didn't want to know that I loved her, or didn't care? Her eyes searched my face, fresh tears spilling down her cheeks.

"Sam?" she whispered. "Are you sure? I don't want-"

"I've never been more sure of anything in my life, Chloe. Never. I love you. I want you. Please come home with me."

Her eyes met mine, and I saw something inside her shift. Raising a hand to wipe her cheeks, she said, "I love you too, Sam."

"Thank God," I said, the tightness inside me easing. "If you'd said you didn't, I was going to have to lock you in here until you changed your mind." As I'd hoped she would, Chloe laughed.

"How long did you think that would take?" she asked. I shrugged.

"Not long. I was going to use orgasms." Chloe laughed again and looked around the room.

"Is that how Axel deals with his prisoners?"

"Somehow, I really don't think so," I said. I sat up, pulling Chloe with me. "Let's go home."

CHAPTER TWELVE
Chloe

I was quiet on the way home, still reeling from everything Sam had said. I'd been so sure I'd understood what he meant when he was talking to Daniel, and then he'd been so weird that morning when I'd asked him about it. But he couldn't have been any clearer in the safe room. He loved me. It was my wildest dream come true. I couldn't quite get my head around it. I'd gotten used to loving Sam, but I'd never expected him to love me back.

He held my hand in his as he drove, every so often looking over at me as if to make sure I was all right. When we were almost to his house he said,

"I hope it's okay, but Dylan and Leigha are coming over for dinner. I asked him a while ago, and I would've canceled, but I thought you needed a distraction. They won't stay late. We need to get some sleep tonight."

"It's fine," I said, not sure if it was fine at all. I knew Dylan. He was a nice guy. But I didn't know his new girlfriend at all. I wasn't sure I wanted to spend the evening with one of the glamour girls these guys usually dated. I was feeling a little too beat up from the events of the last few days and I didn't think my self-esteem could take the hit.

Sam squeezed my hand and looked over at me as we turned through the gates to his house. "Trust me, honey. You'll have fun and we'll make it a short night."

I was doubtful, but I didn't want to get into an argument about it. Sam was thinking of me, trying to be nice. I'd get through the evening one way or another. Though I had to admit the thought of crawling in bed and sleeping for twelve hours or so was very appealing.

I'd been running on adrenaline for most of the day, and the nap in Axel's safe room hadn't refreshed me so much as it had reminded me how tired I was.

Dylan and Leigha arrived only a few minutes after we did. They entered with their arms loaded with white, loop handled shopping bags, trailing delicious scents behind them.

Dylan nodded at me and called out a hello as he headed straight for the kitchen and began unloading containers into the warming oven. Leigha came behind him, trying to balance several bags and a box.

"I'm Chloe," I said, taking the box out of her hands so she could rescue the slipping bags. She smiled at me, a dazzling smile that lit her gray eyes from within.

"I'm Leigha," she said. "And I'm soooo glad to meet you! I've heard so much about you from the boys."

It would be an understatement to say I was surprised to meet her. She was the exact opposite of what I was expecting. Taller than me, but not model tall, she had long dark shining hair, beautiful eyes, and was all curves - full figured and dressed to show it off. She wore a knee length scoop neck suit dress with an A-line skirt and low heels that suggested she might have come straight from work. Though, when she shrugged out of the matching jacket, the dress looked a little more cocktail and a little less office. In a pale shade somewhere between violet and pink, the color was the perfect foil for her gray eyes and dark hair.

Sam and Dylan were conferring over the food, then Sam left saying something about wine. Leigha turned to me and said, "I'm starving. I missed lunch when a client had an emergency and I never got a chance to get a snack. Which would've been fine if I hadn't skipped breakfast too."

Dylan pulled her close with an arm around her waist and kissed her temple, saying, "I keep telling you not to skip breakfast." Looking at me he said,

"On weekends I take her out, or we eat in," this with a sneaking look at Leigha that made her blush, "But on weekdays she always oversleeps and then rushes out without eating. Anyway, who has an accounting emergency?"

"A very old client who has a problem keeping her receipts in order. It was more complicated than that, but I don't want to talk about it. I spent all day untangling the mess and I want wine."

"Sam's getting the wine," Dylan said. "I just have to take out the appetizers."

He unloaded one of the bags on the kitchen island and began to take the covers off the plastic containers. I grabbed a few serving plates from the cabinet and together the three of us laid out the food.

"What is all this?" I asked, my mouthwatering at the spread of treats.

"Lump crab cakes. The rustic platter with pâté, prosciutto, salami, cheeses, and grilled bread." He pointed at each in turn, then went on, "Calamari. And a caprese salad."

"This looks amazing," I said.

"He got a bunch of different things for dinner, too," Leigha said. "The linguine pescatore is for me, but I think there's lasagna, a linguine alla carbonara, something with chicken in it, and then another pasta dish with scallops, I can't remember what it's called. And chocolate decadence cake for dessert."

I hummed under my breath at the thought of dessert. I loved chocolate, especially chocolate cake. Who didn't love chocolate cake? But after a day like this, it sounded like heaven. Sam came back in the room carrying four bottles of wine, two white and two red.

We grabbed the plates and brought them into the great room, setting them on the long coffee table in the center of the seating area. Before I could sit, Sam took my hand and tugged me onto the love seat beside him.

"White or red?" He asked.

"Red," I said. A minute later he was pressing a wine glass into my hand. He sat back and curled his arm around me. I took a sip of the wine, letting the smooth, complex flavor roll over my tongue. I wasn't a wine connoisseur, but I knew that this was much better than the wine I normally bought at the grocery store.

Sam reached over and snagged a small plate on which Leigha had arranged a selection of the appetizers. Grabbing my feet, he pulled them up on his lap and set the plate on my legs. It was a far more casual position than I would normally be in, considering we had guests, one of whom I'd just met. When I would have moved my legs to sit back up, Sam caught me with a look and said,

"Relax." He fed me a bite of one of the crab cakes and my protest was drowned out by the flavor of mustard, spice, and shellfish. The food was so good, I forgot to argue.

Inwardly, I shrugged. It wasn't like this was a business dinner. Dylan was one of Sam's oldest friends. And Leigha didn't seem like she'd be judging me if I wasn't the perfect hostess. Proving me right, she caught my eye and said in a low voice so not to interfere with Sam and Dylan's conversation,

"Don't feel like you have to entertain us. Dylan told me about your brother and everything. I know what it's like to be stressed out and have way too much going on. We'll have plenty of chances to hang out."

"Thanks. I don't mean to be so out of it, it's just-"

She waved a hand at me, dismissing my concerns. "Seriously, I get it. I'm just glad Sam's finally with a cool chick so I have someone to hang with when we all go out. Now we just have to find Axel a woman and we'll be set." Dylan's head swiveled at that. Clearly he hadn't missed our conversation. Giving a light smack to Leigha's hip, he said,

"Do not try to hook Axel up with anyone. Bad idea." Leigha laughed, a bright, clear, happy sound. Her eyes sparkling, she grinned back at Dylan.

"Oh believe me, I wouldn't dare. I can't even imagine the woman who could put up with him. Even though I know he likes me, he still scares me half the time."

Without thinking I said, "He can be very sweet."

Leigha gave me a doubtful look. "He can," I insisted, "in his own Axel way." Sam squeezed his hand on my shoulder getting my attention.

"When was Axel sweet to you? Do I have to go challenge him? Because I can hold my own, but Axel knows things. I'm pretty sure he can kick my ass blindfolded with his hands tied behind his back."

"Axel didn't do anything," I said, smiling at the idea of Axel blindfolded with his hands tied behind his back. Unlike me, I doubted he'd be helpless in that position. But after having had him secure my hands and put a hood over my head, I liked to imagine how he'd feel in the same place. "He talked to me in the van this afternoon. And he was sweet."

I looked up to see Dylan and Leigha looking at me curiously. I shook my head, not ready to explain. Sam leaned over and kissed my temple. "I owe him one," he said.

"Yes, you do," I answered, taking a sip of wine.

I didn't contribute much to the conversation after that, mostly sampled the appetizers and drank my wine. By the time we were ready for dinner, I was on my second glass and getting a little tipsy. I chose the linguine alla carbonara for dinner. Between the wine and the full plate of pasta, my eyes were drooping even before we got to dessert. Dylan and Leigha took their chocolate cake to go, not having to be told that I was about to fall asleep at the table. Leigha gave me a quick hug before she went, promising to get my number from Dylan and call soon.

Sam led me away from the table and back to the love seat in the great room where he pulled me onto his lap, positioning me so I could lean back against the arm of the couch, giving me a perfect view of the skyline of Vegas and the moonlit desert beyond. Leaning forward for a second, he grabbed one of the pieces of cake and a fork from the coffee table.

"Open up," he said, and when I did, he slipped a forkful of chocolate cake between my lips. Rich and sweet, it melted over my tongue. I gave a little moan at how delicious it was. Have I mentioned I love chocolate? We shared the cake, trading bites, not talking.

When it was gone, Sam put the plate on the table and snuggled my head into his shoulder, stroking my hair with his fingertips. I was asleep in minutes.

I didn't wake up when he brought me to bed, or when he undressed me. I vaguely remember turning into him in the night, wrapping my arm over his chest and using his shoulder as a pillow. I slept hard, dreamless and deep, and woke in the morning feeling refreshed.

I was alone in the bed, though I heard Sam in another room, maybe in his office, talking to someone. A glance at the clock told me it wasn't Daniel, he would already be gone. I was just sitting up, pulling the sheet with me, when Sam came in, his face grave, phone in his hand.

"What?" I asked. He tossed the phone on the bed

and stared at me, his blue eyes pained.

"Sergey Tesepov just called me," he said. "He wants a meeting. Now. With you."

the Courtship Maneuver

BOOK THREE

CHAPTER ONE
Chloe

I stared at Sam, my jaw dropped, unable to think past the terrifying insanity of Sergey Tsepov calling a meeting with me.

"How did he get your number?" I asked. It wasn't the most important question, but it was the one that popped into my head first. Sam shook his head.

"I don't know."

"Where are we meeting him? And when?" I asked, getting out of the bed. I wrapped my arms around my waist, suddenly self-conscious about being naked in front of Sam in the bright morning light. His eyes lingering on my curves said that I had nothing to be self-conscious about. Then he gave a light shake of his head as if to push away the distraction of my naked body, and said,

"At a restaurant downtown. Another one of his fronts. He invited us for brunch, just the three of us. Actually, he invited you. I invited myself."

I didn't know what to say to that. I hoped Sam knew there was no way I would've gone without him. I'd been reckless the past few days, that was true, but nowhere near reckless enough to go meet Sergey Tsepov by myself. Not that Sam would have let me anyway.

"Let me jump in the shower," I said. "I'll be ready in a few minutes."

Sam gave me a short nod and said, "I'd join you, but we need to leave as soon as we can, and if I get in that shower with you, there's no way we'll be fast."

A rush of heat blasted through me at the look in his eyes, and I felt my cheeks turn pink. A little embarrassed and not sure how to handle it, I bolted for the bathroom. For the second time in two days I jumped under the water before it had a chance to warm up.

There wasn't time to wash my hair. I twisted it out of the way with a clip and took the fastest shower I could manage. Sam came in while I was shaving my legs and bent over the sink to brush his teeth. The casual intimacy of getting ready together felt oddly comfortable and familiar, steadying my nerves. He left the bathroom to get dressed before I was done, and by the time I entered the closet to pick my clothes Sam was already dressed, standing in front of the mirror, tying his tie.

He'd chosen a dark charcoal suit, with a crisp white shirt, and a patterned blue tie that I'd bought him for his birthday the year before. It had tiny yellow dump trucks printed on it in a cross-hatch pattern. The trucks were indistinguishable from yellow dots unless you were standing right in front of him. Across the board room, or a desk, it looked like any other conservatively fashionable tie. The blue exactly matched Sam's eyes. I couldn't help but smile when I saw it.

Taking my cue from Sam, I dressed for the office. Depending on how things went with Tsepov, we'd most likely be heading there later. I didn't want to give the wrong signals. Especially not to a man as dangerous as Sergey Tsepov. I chose one of the more formal suits in Lola's wardrobe, a lightweight brown and grey heathered tweed with a fitted jacket and trim skirt that fell just below my knees. I paired it with a chocolate silk blouse and matching spiked heel knee-high boots.

The clothes were stylish, and like all of Lola's selections, looked fantastic on me. What they were not was provocative. I'd chosen light makeup and pinned my hair up in a tight bun. By the time we got to brunch, tendrils would have escaped to soften the effect, but it was as business-like a hairstyle as I could manage.

Sam studied my suit and my hair before crossing the room to kiss me, his hand on my cheek, tilting my head up to his.

"You're so beautiful," he said. "In anything you wear, you're beautiful. But I like your hair better down. Except for this. Right now, I'm glad you're wearing it up. I don't want him to see any more of you than he has to."

Taking my hand, he led me out of the bedroom and down the hall. In the kitchen, we grabbed both of our briefcases, as well as my purse, then headed to the garage, our moods grim.

When we were fastening our seat belts I said, "Did he explain why he wants to meet with us?"

"No. Not really. Only that he's been hearing a lot about you, and with the situation concerning Nolan so uncertain, he felt it was in your best interest to meet with him."

"That doesn't tell us anything," I said.

"No, it doesn't. We have backup. While you were in the shower, I called Axel and we've got two guys on us. They'll be watching the building, but we can't take them inside. Still, it's better than nothing."

I didn't answer. I was too busy trying to take deep breaths and calm the panic growing in my chest. I did not want to meet with Sergey Tsepov. I wanted my brother to come home and everything to go back to normal. Not Sam and me. I didn't want to change a thing about our new relationship. But I wanted the rest of this mess to just go away. It was a child's dream, the hope that life could rewind itself and somehow match my vision of happiness.

Even at its best, life never painted the pictures in our heads. Sometimes the surprises were good. My most hopeful imaginings wouldn't have dreamed up the words Sam had said to me in the safe room the day before. And my most desperate wishes couldn't make Nolan the man I wanted him to be. I was going to have to learn to live with that. Still, I dreaded hearing what Tsepov would have to say.

From the outside, Tsepov's place looked like any other sophisticated restaurant. Through the front windows I caught sight of white linen tablecloths and dark polished wood. Sam was lifting his hand to knock on the front door when it swung open and a waiter in a tuxedo waved us in with a flourish. Sam kept his hand on my arm, angling his body between mine and the open dining room. The space was mostly empty, the tables in various states of readiness for the afternoon lunch service.

The waiter who opened the door led us through the dining room in silence. I caught the sound of voices coming through the swinging door to the kitchen and the clank of silverware as it was rolled in napkins. We went down a hall, past the coat room, and turned into a private dining room. It would've been perfectly at home in an English country house, with creamy walls and heavy, dark wainscoting below the chair rail. Oil paintings of hunting parties hung around the room and over the gas fireplace, lit with a cheerful flame. At the head of the long, rectangular table sat a man who could only be Sergey Tsepov.

CHAPTER TWO
Chloe

He didn't rise when we entered, but held out a hand in welcome waving us toward his end of the table where two places had been set, one on either side of him. Though I didn't want to separate from Sam, it didn't seem wise to make a fuss. Squeezing his hand, I pulled my arm free and walked down the opposite side of the table to our host. When I reached Tsepov, I held out my hand.

I expected him to shake it. Instead he brought it to his lips and kissed the backs of my fingers. I fought the urge to shudder. He wasn't unattractive. Actually, he was far more attractive than I'd expected. I couldn't tell since he hadn't stood, but he looked tall. Maybe Sam's height. Leaner than Sam, his shoulders not quite as broad, with an elegant build that matched the perfect bone structure of his face. He was older, maybe Daniel's age, and he wore it well, the white at his temples contrasting with his thick dark hair, giving him a dashing look. Despite all of that, even if I hadn't known who he was, I would have shied away.

He wore menace like a cloak over his well tailored suit. Nothing like Axel, who I'd always thought a little scary. With Axel there was a certainty, underneath it all, that he was a good man. You might not always like what he did, but he wore his ethics like a suit of armor. Sergey Tsepov was nothing like that. Beneath his charm he was ice cold. This was a man who would do what he had to, or what he wanted to, no matter the cost. This was not a man I wanted to cross.

"Please, sit," he said, indicating our places with a dictator's benevolence. "Thank you for coming at such short notice."

I sat. Sam took his seat across from me, his eyes on mine both cautioning and concerned. I didn't need the warning to be careful. I was done with being reckless. And even if I got another wild hair, I wouldn't be doing anything stupid in front of Tsepov. At least, not if I could help it. I sensed Tsepov was waiting for me to speak, but since I had no idea what to say, I kept my mouth shut. After waiting a beat, he stepped into the silence.

"So you are Chloe Henson." I nodded, though it seemed unnecessary. His eyes crawled over me, polite and assessing. Beneath the surface something predatory lurked, cataloging every weakness to use to his advantage. "Your brother spoke of you. He had much to say, mostly complaints, but it is clear he loves you. It is always the way of the young to complain, is it not? We do our best for them and they see only restriction and limits. So rarely do they appreciate how they need these limits."

Again, I nodded. It hurt to hear that Nolan had complained about me, but I wasn't surprised. I wondered if Tsepov had a child of his own who complained about his parental concern. Oddly I felt a moment of kinship with him. I knew Nolan loved me. And I also knew I drove him nuts with my mothering. Though, if he hated it that much, he was always welcome to save up some money and get his own place. Since he'd never bothered to move out, he couldn't find me as burdensome as he said he did.

"What can we do for you?" Sam asked, his tone firm but respectful. Tsepov moved his attention from me and I relaxed a little.

"You are Ms. Henson's employer? Sam Logan, owner and CEO of Desert Vistas Development. I believe we almost did business together at one time."

"Yes," Sam said. "Chloe works for me. We also have a personal relationship."

"Which explains much about your interest in her brother's troubles," Tsepov said.

"We haven't been able to find out much about Nolan," I said, the tension between Sam and Tsepov making me nervous.

"Then we share a problem. Tell me what you know," Tsepov said, his words a polite demand, but a demand none the less. I looked at Sam and he sent me a tiny nod.

"We heard that he lost money at poker and is in debt to you. That he's been working for you, using his skills on the computer. And that you asked him to do a job, he disappeared, and the last person who saw him is dead."

"Then sadly, you know only a little less than I do myself."

Tsepov looked up as two waiters entered the room carrying covered plates. A third followed behind, holding a tray with delicate cups and saucers, along with a sterling silver coffee pot. Conversation halted as they served us. If I'd had any appetite I would have been thrilled by the meal before me. Eggs Benedict, covered in rich, lemony hollandaise, thick cut bacon, and a precise circle of crispy home fries.

"Eat," Tsepov ordered with a wave of his hand. I added cream and sugar to my coffee and drank before lifting my fork and stabbing a piece of potato.

"You have Axel Sinclair looking for Nolan," Tsepov stated flatly. Sam nodded. "I do not like Axel Sinclair nosing around my business. Call him off."

"Our only concern is locating Chloe's brother," Sam said, his eyes hard. "We have no interest in your business."

"Nolan is my business." Tsepov sliced into his

eggs with a quick slash of his knife. The golden yolk running across his plate should have been appetizing, but his aggression turned my stomach. The ice beneath his friendly demeanor made it too easy to imagine him slicing into a human as casually as he cut into his eggs.

"Surely you can see how he is also Chloe's business," Sam said and took a bite of his eggs. Tsepov turned his attention back to me.

"I appreciate loyalty. Your care for your brother is commendable. If he has remained loyal to me, he will be taken care of and those who have troubled him will be punished."

"And if he's made a mistake?" I asked, a tremor in my voice. Tsepov's gaze turned to cold steel.

"There is no room for mistakes. And no second chances." He ate with single-minded attention for several minutes. The conversation clearly at a halt, Sam and I did the same. When Tsepov put down his silverware and picked up his coffee, he resumed speaking as if there had been no break. "Has Sinclair determined the nature of Nolan's last job?"

"None of the specifics," Sam said shaking his head. "Only enough to know that the rumor is Nolan succeeded in acquiring the information that you wanted, but that he has not delivered it. To anyone."

"And have you heard any talk about his intentions?" Tsepov asked in a silkily dangerous tone.

"Some. The consensus seems to be that he is loyal," Sam said, "or not stupid enough to betray you. We haven't been able to find anyone who can confirm that he's made an offer to deliver the information to anyone else. Our best guess is that he is hiding out and for some reason is unable to get to you."

Tsepov looked to the door which remained closed, his eyes shuttered, impossible to read. "You are implying I have a weakness in my organization," he said, finally.

"I'm only telling you what we've heard. As you know, there are two options. Nolan has decided to betray you and is looking for another buyer. Or Nolan's loyal but unable to complete his assignment."

"And what do you think?" Tsepov asked, pinning me with his stare. I tensed under his focused gaze.

"I think that there's a lot about my brother I don't know," I admitted. "But I don't believe he's betrayed you."

"Sentiment?" Tsepov asked, shaking his head, already dismissing my answer.

"No," I said. "Logic. There are a lot of people looking for Nolan. If he was attempting to broker some kind of deal, word would've gotten out. Instead there's only speculation and more questions. That makes me think he's keeping his head down until whatever has him scared goes away. Nolan's always been like that. He doesn't like confrontation. If things get difficult, he runs away."

Tsepov looked away again, seemingly lost in thought. I wasn't foolish enough to comment that all signs pointed to someone in his own organization as the problem. Only someone close to Tsepov would be able to intercept Nolan and his attempts to get the information to his boss. Tsepov was smart enough to have figured that out, and I wasn't going to be the one to throw it in his face.

"I will allow you to continue to use Sinclair's services in pursuit of Nolan, out of respect for Ms. Henson's familial responsibility. If that interference causes me trouble in the future, I will hold you both responsible. Is that understood?" Tsepov asked, folding his hands on the table before him.

"It is," Sam said.

"I suggest," Tsepov went on, "That Mr. Sinclair find Nolan before I do. And if Nolan has made any regrettable decisions, you change his mind."

"We will," Sam said.

At this, Tsepov's eyes landed on me one last time. "Ms. Henson, a piece of advice. A woman such as yourself must be careful. You have been exposed to men who will not take care with you. Do you understand?" I nodded, my throat dry. "Mr. Logan has taken responsibility for you. Allow him to do this. Allow him to keep you out of trouble. Until this regrettable situation, Nolan was a valued employee. My hope is that once he is located he will continue to be my valued employee. It is out of regard for that relationship that I tell you this; Let your man look for your brother. Until Nolan is back in my fold, I cannot extend myself to protect you. Don't make it necessary for me to wish that I had."

I nodded again, not quite sure exactly what he'd meant, but scared all the same. Sam pushed back his chair and rose. I did the same.

"Thank you for making the time to see us," Sam said. Tsepov nodded his head and said,

"Find him before I do, Mr. Logan."

CHAPTER THREE
Chloe

My knees were shaking as we left the restaurant, my heart pounding so hard the sound filled my ears. Although Tsepov hadn't been anything but gracious, I had the feeling that we had just escaped a deadly threat.

We got in the truck and buckled in. Sam didn't speak, just put the car in gear and then took my hand in his. I wondered if he was as rattled as I was. Based on the hard set of his jaw, and the tight clasp of his hand, I thought he might be.

"When we find your brother," Sam said through gritted teeth, "I'm going to kill him."

"Sam!" I said in protest.

"Do you think I'm kidding?" Sam looked at me his eyes blazing with anger and something else that could have been fear. "We just a breakfast with a Russian mob boss who told you to let me keep you out of trouble because you were attracting the wrong attention. And the only reason we were there at all, or that any dangerous attention is on you, is because of your brother. Did you miss the part where Tsepov said that Nolan would continue to work for him?"

I hadn't missed that. And I was guessing you didn't just quit your job when you worked for someone like Sergey Tsepov.

"I know this is all Nolan's fault. I'm not defending him. But I can't turn my back on my brother. He's my only family."

"He's going to get you killed."

"I hope not," I said, trying for a joke. The murderous look Sam gave me said I hadn't been funny. "Sorry," I said. "But can we argue about what to do with Nolan *after* we find him?"

"Why not?" Sam asked his tone inappropriately amused. "If we don't find him, or the wrong people find him first, they'll kill him and save me the trouble."

Maybe I should've yelled at Sam for being so flippant about Nolan's chances. I couldn't bring myself to say anything. He was right. Ending up with the terrifying man we'd just left was looking like Nolan's best case scenario. I wasn't sure what to do about that. I suspected there was nothing I *could* do about it.

To save my sanity, I decided to focus on work. I hadn't been in the office at all the day before, and my desk would likely be a disaster. I was right, it was.

One of my most essential functions at Desert Vistas Development was to form a wall between Sam and everyone else. Without me as a go-between, people would be in and out of his office all the time and he wouldn't get anything done. Part of it was his own fault for being so hands on with the company, but he'd built it from a single trailer on a tiny project into the thriving business it was today. While he'd learned to delegate, he couldn't help paying attention to all the small details.

Everyone ignored my inbox. They piled notes, files, all sorts of things on my desk, asking me to put them in front of Sam. After I made us coffee, I began to sort through the mess. I hadn't been at it more than a few minutes when my speakerphone beeped and I heard Sam's voice say, "Chloe? Would you come in here for a minute please?"

I got up and went into his office, bringing in notepad and a pen with me. I'd barely cleared the door, when his hand closed over my wrist and he yanked me through, shutting and locking it behind me. I looked up at him in surprise, opening my mouth to protest. I didn't get very far.

Before I could think of what to say, he was kissing me, his arms holding me tight his tongue stroking mine in fierce possession. By the time he let me go, my knees were weak, and I sagged against him.

"Sam," I whispered into his shirt. "We can't do this at the office." He nuzzled the top of my head with his chin.

"I know. I know," he said. "Just this once. Maybe twice."

I pulled back and swatted his chest. "Sam, I'm serious. I love you, but I don't want to get a reputation as the secretary who's sleeping with the boss. Okay?"

"Okay. Really, okay. I get it, and I don't want anyone to think that about you, either. At least not the way you mean. I'll learn to control myself, somehow."

I straightened my jacket and brushed my hands over my hips smoothing the skirt. The suit was beautifully tailored and looked great on me, but it made me look like an elegant and stylish librarian. Not someone who would inspire sudden fits of passion in the office. It gave me a thrill to know I'd done that anyway, just by being me. Trying to focus on the business at hand, I picked up the notebook and pen from where I'd dropped them on the floor and said, "Did you need me for any actual work?"

"Yes, I did."

Pointedly, I opened the office door and left it that way before I took a seat on the other side of Sam's desk and waited, my pen poised over the notebook. It was almost an hour before I left his office with another huge to-do list on top of the one I had from earlier in the week, none of which could be addressed until I dealt with the mess still covering my desk. This was why I never took vacations.

Normally, I was the one who reminded Sam

about lunch, but I was neck deep in work and after our late breakfast, lunch slipped my mind. Sam called me at my desk and asked me to put in an order for something. I called out for delivery, already knowing what he'd want. I worked for a little longer, my desk finally organized once more and almost three quarters of the way through my original to do list. I looked up from my work at the sound of feet on the hardwood floor, expecting to see our lunch delivery.

Instead, it was Jack from our legal department. He held a thick copy of what looked like the set of contracts we'd reviewed earlier in the week. Glancing between me and the closed door to Sam's office he said, "Is he in a meeting? Or do you think I could stick my head in for a minute?"

"I think it's probably fine, Jack. He's just about to break for lunch anyway," I said smiling up at him. Looking at the contracts in his hand I asked, "Do you need copies of those to leave with him?"

Jack held them out to me. "Do you mind? The copier down in legal is jammed, and I didn't want to wait."

I shook my head, saying, "No problem." Taking the contracts from Jack, I crossed the room to put them on the copier, hitting the buttons to make a second set. "You can go on in, Jack. I'll bring these in a second."

I expected Jack to let himself into Sam's office, but instead he stood there, watching me at the copier.

Looking back over my shoulder as the copier shuffled and flashed, I caught Jack's eye and raised my eyebrows. He cleared his throat and took a step closer, shoving his hands in his pockets.

"I'll wait," he said, clearing his throat again. Then, after a minute of awkward silence, he said, "You look different, Chloe. I mean, you look good."

"Thanks, Jack," I said, a little confused. I thought I looked nice in my new clothes, but it wasn't like Jack to say anything.

"Would you go out to dinner with me?" He straightened his shoulders and met my eyes when I turned to look at him. I opened my mouth to answer, then snapped it shut at the sight of Sam standing in the open doorway, his blue eyes narrowed tightly on Jack.

"No," Sam said, clearly aggravated. "She would not like to have dinner with you. She's having dinner with me. Tonight. And every other night."

I glared at Sam. That was not subtle. And that was definitely not keeping our relationship quiet. I ground my teeth, taking the finished copies and handing them to Jack with an apologetic look. Anything I said at this point would only make it worse, so I kept my mouth shut as Sam said to Jack,

"In my office."

The door shut behind them and I sighed, sitting down and resting my forehead on my desk. When had my life gotten so complicated?

CHAPTER FOUR
Sam

Chloe was pissed. So was I, but that wasn't her fault. Or Jack's. The sight of them, Chloe looking beautiful and surprised, and Jack eyeing her with that hungry stare, was just too much. Especially after the pool hall and the bar. I didn't think I could take watching any more men lusting after my woman. Maybe when we'd been together longer I'd find it funny, or entertaining. I wasn't there yet.

Now that she was wearing her new clothes, every other man could see what I already knew. That she was luscious, all abundant curves, and smooth soft skin. Warm eyes and gorgeous hair. Sweet full lips and perfect legs. I wanted her to feel good about herself, to see the same beauty that I saw when she looked in the mirror. I hadn't thought about everyone else seeing it, too.

I sat behind my desk and waited for Jack to take a seat across from me. He shrugged and met my eyes with a helpless grin.

"Sorry, man," he said propping his ankle up on his knee. "I always liked Chloe, but I never realized she was so hot. I thought I'd better take a shot before someone else did."

"I already got there," I said, reigning in my temper with effort. Jack had worked for me for seven years. We were friends. He was a good guy. None of that stopped me from wanting to punch him for calling Chloe hot. Even though she was. Jealousy was a bitch.

"I see that," Jack said, easily, raising his hands up in front of him in a gesture of innocence. "Won't happen again."

"Don't say anything to anyone. Not yet."

"What do you mean?" Jack asked, his eyes suddenly intent on me. "Is this just some secret office fling? Because that's not why *I* asked her out."

"No," I said, with more force than necessary. "No. It's serious. But she's skittish about anyone at work knowing. She doesn't want people to think less of her for getting involved with me. So don't tell anyone until she figures out how she wants to handle it, okay?"

"No, that's cool," Jack said, relaxing into his chair. "No one would think less of her. She's the only reason most of us can put up with you. But I can keep my mouth shut."

"Thanks," I said. "Now show me what's changed in these contracts so I can have lunch with Chloe."

He did, taking me through the adjustments with

the focused efficiency I was used to in Jack. We were done twenty minutes later. I walked him out, stopping at the door to my office, glad to see a brown paper bag on Chloe's desk, still stapled shut, beside two styrofoam cups. She couldn't be that mad if she'd waited for me before eating lunch.

Jack gave Chloe a wink and a jaunty wave as he left the executive suite, but didn't try to start a conversation. Smart man. Then again, if he hadn't been, I wouldn't have hired him. His invitation to Chloe had my mind racing. Normally I was the last guy to rush toward commitment.

Who was I kidding? Normally I didn't know the meaning of the word commitment, at least where women were concerned. Chloe wasn't just any woman. She was the only woman for me. I'd have to move this forward, make a public statement she could live with, or I'd be chasing off every unattached guy in the company. And there were a lot of them.

Chloe stood as I neared her desk, picking up the paper bag and styrofoam cups. Without a word, she marched past me into my office, her back straight, chin high. Yep. I was in trouble. Damn.

I followed her back into the office, closing and locking the door behind us. She heard the lock flick into place and her head whipped around.

"Sam, unlock that door."

"Not right now," I said. "I want to eat lunch without anyone interrupting."

"If anyone comes, they'll think-"

I shook my head, cutting her off. "They won't. You only think they will because you feel guilty. You have nothing to feel guilty about, honey. We're both adults, both free to be together, and this is our lunch hour. Leave the door alone and eat."

She sighed, and the stiffness went out of her spine. She started to sit on the chair opposite my desk, where she usually sat when we worked or ate lunch together, but I stopped her.

"Over here," I said, grabbing the bag and going to the leather couch on the far side of my office. I rarely used the sitting area. Most of the time I was at my desk if I was in the office. Chloe and I had never eaten over there, even though it was more comfortable than the desk. It had never occurred to me, probably not to her either. But we'd been apart for the past few hours and I missed her. I didn't want to sit across the desk, I wanted her beside me.

She sat down, smoothing her skirt over her legs and crossing her feet at the ankles, knees together. Now that I knew what it was like to have her in bed, her prim manner turned me on even more. Anyone looking at her would think she was too buttoned up to be the same woman who'd writhed beneath me, begging me to fuck her. And no one else would ever know. Chloe was mine. Forever.

CHAPTER FIVE
Chloe

I smoothed my skirt over my legs, a little nervous about being alone with Sam in his office with the door locked. It was silly. We ate in here all the time, though not on the couch. And we'd had the door closed and locked before when we'd worked on sensitive projects. It didn't happen often, but it wasn't completely unusual. I was just off balance and everything felt weird.

Sam sat down beside me and opened the bag with our lunch. His turkey sandwich and my tuna melt. Wordlessly, he slid his wrapped pickle my way. Sam didn't like pickles. Whenever we got deli sandwiches for lunch, he always gave me his pickle.

At the way that sounded in my head I giggled. *Sam gave me his pickle.* He sure did. I giggled again. For a responsible adult, I could be so immature. Or maybe it was just the stress getting to me. Sam handed me my iced tea and gave me an odd look.

"Something funny?" he asked.

I shook my head, but kept giggling, unable to stop, the grave concern on his face setting me off even worse. I put the drink down on the coffee table before I spilled it and braced my forearms on my knees, dropping my head to hide my face. I was over the stupid pickle joke, but I kept giggling, my laughs abruptly changing to sobs as tears streamed down my face. What was wrong with me?

Sam put his food down and pulled me into his arms, tucking my hair behind my ear and kissing my forehead. "Shhh, honey. It's okay. Shhh."

I gasped for breath, fighting the sobs I couldn't seem to control and said, "Sorry. Sorry, Sam. I don't know what's wrong with me."

"I do, honey. You're under a lot of stress and trying to pretend everything is okay. You're scared for Nolan. It's normal to be freaking out a little. It's okay."

"I'm not like this. I don't cry all the time. I'm not like Melissa," I said, talking about a woman in our Marketing department who was known for bursting into tears at the drop of a hat. I went out of my way to be nice to her, but sometimes I wanted to tell her to pull herself together. And here I was, bawling for what felt like the millionth time this week.

"Not the same, Clo. I've known you three years and I don't think I've ever seen you cry. Not until this thing with Nolan. Don't worry about it. You're due."

He squeezed me against his chest and continued to rub my back, soothing me until I calmed down and my breath evened out.

I sat up and wiped my face, using the napkins on the table to clean away my smudged eyeliner. Our surreal breakfast with Sergey Tsepov was finally starting to sink in. I looked at Sam and said,

"Nolan isn't going to be able to get clear of this, is he?" Sam hesitated, as if he was trying to decide how much of the truth to tell me. "Be honest," I said. He shook his head.

"I can't tell the future, Clo. Maybe if he squares up with Tsepov, he could let some time go by and then quietly leave town, start over somewhere else. But that depends on how much Tsepov wants to keep him."

"Do you think Nolan betrayed Tsepov?" I asked.

"I have no idea. And neither do you. Even smart people do stupid shit sometimes. He could have. But there are enough people in this that he could also be a victim of someone else's scheme. We just don't know."

I didn't respond. I wanted so desperately to believe that Nolan wouldn't be stupid enough to steal from Tsepov. But Sam was right. People did stupid things all the time. Look at the way I'd gone to that bar to find Sam and confront Dog. Anyone who knew me probably would have sworn I'd never do something that crazy. *I* would have sworn it if you'd asked me the day before. Yet, fueled by anger and frustration, I'd walked right in to the last place I should have been. Who knew what Nolan might have done with the right motivation?

"I just want to find him so this can be over," I said, mostly to myself. Sam handed me my sandwich and said,

"So do I. Axel is working on it. Hopefully he'll turn up something soon."

I nodded and unwrapped my lunch. I'd lost my appetite after all the crying, but I ate it anyway, knowing I'd be hungry later if I didn't. When we were finished, I went to pack up the trash, but Sam got to it first, shoving the sandwich wrappings in the bag and stacking the cups inside one another. For once, I ignored the pickles, opting for one of the red and pink mints at the bottom of the bag. I crunched it between my teeth, letting the sweet bite of mint wash the tuna out of my mouth. I loved tuna melts, but the aftertaste wasn't the best.

"I'm not ready to get back to work, yet," he said. I glanced at the clock across the room. One thirty. We were running behind and still had a lot to do before the end of the day. I started to protest when he took my hand and tugged, pulling me back onto the couch beside him.

"We should-"

"I know. We will." His blue eyes roamed my face. "We won't make a habit of this, I promise."

I leaned into him, my lips meeting his half way. I agreed. We couldn't make this a habit. But I was calling for an exception, just this one time. I needed Sam. And maybe he needed me, too.

Sam drew me into his arms, and I tried to get closer, but my tight skirt pinned my knees together, making movement awkward. Aggravated, and only wanting Sam, I stood up, looking down into his surprised eyes. "One second," I said.

I wiggled my hips a little and began to hike up my skirt. Sam's eyes widened comically, heat filling them as I bared the tops of my brown leather boots, then my thighs. The spike heels of the boots tilted my hips forward, making my legs and butt look perkier than usual. The boots were the only part of my outfit that was openly sexy. They lent me the boost of confidence I needed to give Sam a saucy smile and climb onto his lap, taking his face in my hands as I claimed his mouth with a kiss.

So far it had always been Sam initiating things between us. Now it was my turn. I wasn't going to be the passive partner in this relationship. Sam may have had more experience, but I had enthusiasm. I had love. And plenty of pent up desire.

I threw myself into the kiss, sinking my fingers into the thick, blond silk of his hair, tugging gently to bring him even closer. His arms came around me, pulling me tight to his chest, one hand dropping to cup my ass and squeeze. Then both his hands were on my ass, dragging me tight against him, working their way beneath my skirt, which wasn't hard since it was nearly at my waist.

When his fingertips slid beneath my lace panties to graze my heated pussy, I gasped into his mouth. I kissed him harder, the liquid pleasure between my legs making my head spin. He got me hot so fast, all it took was the smallest touches, and I was hungry for more. One long finger teased my entrance, sinking in just a bit before sliding out and tracing a circle, then dipping back in again. Teasing me. Making me moan with need.

Even my most heated fantasies of Sam hadn't included having sex with him in his office. My imagination hadn't dared to go that far. But there was one thing that had crept into my secret dreams. I'd always envisioned doing it at his desk, my body hidden beneath the bulky furniture while he lounged back in his chair and let me pleasure him.

The couch would do well enough. Peeking over my shoulder to reassure myself that the door was safely closed, though I already knew it was locked, I slid off Sam's lap. He murmured a protest, but I ignored him. I stood before him in my proper suit, the power of his need flowing through me, making me brave. Taking a step back, I raised my hands and began to unbutton my jacket. Sam froze in the middle of reaching for me and slowly sat back. I bit my lip, looking down at his face, his blue eyes burning, the flush of passion on his cheekbones. He was mine. And I was going to show him how much I wanted him.

The last button of the jacket undone, I shrugged it off my shoulders and tossed it onto a nearby arm chair. I thought for a second, then dropped my hands to the back of my skirt and undid the single button at my waist. A tug on the zipper, a shimmy of my hips and the conservative tweed skirt fell to the floor. I stepped out of it and bent over, flashing Sam a view of my breasts through the gaping neckline of my blouse as I picked up the skirt and tossed it on top of the jacket.

Now I was standing in front of him wearing only the spike heel, knee-high boots, a thin blouse the color of bitter-sweet chocolate and matching lace underwear. I swayed my hips to music only I could hear and unbuttoned the blouse, taking my time with each button. Sam sat frozen on the couch, his eyes riveted to my hands, his cock rock hard and pressing against his charcoal gray suit pants. His breath came in short, quiet bursts, everything about him completely still. I imagined he was afraid any sudden moves might break the spell and scare me off.

That wasn't going to happen. I was on a mission and Sam was my goal. Well, Sam and his cock. They were both all mine. I finally got the last button and peeled the blouse off, one shoulder at a time, letting it drop to catch on my elbows before I sent it flying to land with the rest of my clothes. My bra followed a second later. I was getting too impatient to tease. I hooked my thumbs in my panties, but lost my nerve. It was enough to be mostly naked, wearing only the knee-high boots and nearly transparent lace panties.

Dropping to my knees, I reached for Sam's belt. He got there before me, spreading his knees and unfastening the belt and his pants. I rose up between his legs, hands trembling, eager to touch him. His cock pushed free of the smothering fabric as soon as his zipper was down, reaching for me, wanting my touch as much as I needed to give it.

I was clumsy. Sam didn't seem to care. He sucked in a sharp breath when my mouth closed over the head of his cock. I licked up the bead of pre-come, savoring the salty taste of him. He was big, almost too much to fit. I breathed through my nose, relaxing my jaw and sinking down, taking him deeper, stroking his skin, loving the feel of it, satin over steel and so alive. For me. Just for me.

There was no way I could fit all of him in my mouth. Maybe with practice. Not my first time. Remembering a conversation with a girl-friend about oral sex that had left me blushing and sent my imagination running wild, I reached up to wrap my fingers around the length of Sam's cock that I hadn't managed to fit in my mouth. He was slick from my attentions, and my fingers slipped easily over him, my grip firm, matching the rhythm of my lips as they rose and fell.

His fingers sank into my hair, not guiding me, just along for the ride, his grip a possessive caress that sent my rising desire soaring. Groaning as I gave a hard suck, he shifted forward, spreading his legs wider, giving me more room. I rose higher on my knees, coming down from above, taking him an inch deeper.

"Oh, God. Chloe." That was it. Just, "Chloe." He said my name again, his hips shifting under my weight, pumping into my mouth in tiny pulses I knew he tried to hold back. The power of it was intoxicating. This strong man was losing control because of something I was doing. He needed me so much that he was almost helpless from my touch.

Almost, but not completely. With a harsh, pained groan, Sam tightened his fingers in my hair and pulled me away with a gentle, firm pressure. Uncertain, I let him, wondering if I'd been doing something wrong. The questions flew from my mind. He lifted me from the floor and tossed me to the couch on my back, flipping on top of me, settling himself between my legs. More than ready for him, I raised my knees back, opening to him, needing him to fill my pussy as he had my mouth.

He sat back just long enough to yank my panties down my legs. A breath later and he was pressing inside, careful to go slowly. I was wet and ready, but still too tight for him to take me the way I wanted him to. Short, maddening thrusts of him inside me, filling me inch by inch, the stretch a little pain, mostly pleasure. I squeezed my eyes tight, tipping my head back, my hips tilting up to his, taking him in.

"Sam," I moaned into his ear, "Sam, harder. Please, harder."

He gave me what I wanted as he filled me completely, pulling halfway out and driving back in, the jolt of pleasure startling a short scream from me. It was so good. Too good. I was going to come before we really got started. Sam must have felt me tighten around him, because he said in a guttural whisper, "That's right, honey. Come for me. Come on my cock. Let me feel it."

I did, my pussy clamping down as he fucked me, squeezing him in rhythmic clenches that stole my breath. Before my scream could escape my mouth and give us away, he kissed me, sealing his lips to mine, silencing my cries of pleasure.

CHAPTER SIX
Chloe

I held tight to Sam until the aftershocks of my orgasm had passed, unwilling to let go. It took me a minute to remember where we were. I blushed when Sam rolled us over, almost tipping us off the couch in the process. I ended up on top of him, straddling his hips, nuzzling his neck and drifting in a haze, right up until I heard a short knock on the office door, followed by a rattle of the handle. Thankfully, it was still locked.

Voices echoed in the outer office, then faded away. "Sam," I whispered, horrified. "Sam, they almost came in."

"Love, the door is locked. No one can get in." He was laughing, just a little, at my sudden attack of propriety after I'd stripped almost naked and made my first attempt at a blow job right in his office.

"I know," I hissed in a nearly silent tone, though

whoever had tried to come in was long gone. "But still, what if they had?"

"Chloe, look at me."

I did, scowling at the glint of amusement in his blue eyes.

"I would never let that happen, honey. I swear. Never. Okay?"

I nodded. I knew he wouldn't. It just freaked me out, being naked except for my boots, tangled up with Sam, who was still mostly in his suit, and hearing people trying the door. Reason number one not to do this in the office again. My nerves would never survive the shock of almost being caught a second time. Giving him a quick kiss on his stubbled jaw, I shot to my feet, snatched my clothes from the chair where I'd thrown them, and dashed for Sam's private bathroom.

He'd need it too, but he'd have to wait a second. At least he was still mostly dressed. I cleaned up and pulled my clothes back on as quickly as I could, biting my lip in further embarrassment when the bathroom door cracked open a few inches to admit Sam's hand, my lace panties dangling from his extended finger.

"Thanks," I yelped, slamming the door so fast he barely had time to get his hand out of the way. I was done a few minutes later, emerging to find Sam looking as if nothing had happened, only the satisfied glint in his eyes giving him away. My hair pins were lined up in a row on his desk. I'd been in such a rush to get my clothes back on, I'd forgotten my hair. So much for the bun. There was no way I'd get it back up without my brush, which was in my purse in the outer office.

"I have sex hair," I said to Sam, finger combing it, trying to get the curls and waves to behave.

"Yes, but only I know. Everyone else will just think you look good with your hair down."

I looked at him doubtfully. "Really?"

"Really," he said, kissing me lightly on the lips. "You look completely innocent. I swear."

I stared at him, wanting another kiss, knowing I needed to get back to my desk before I pushed my luck too far. Someone always needed one of us. I steeled myself to face the rest of the office and unlocked the door, swinging it open with faked nonchalance, my heart racing. To my everlasting relief, the outer office was empty, everything as I'd left it except for a yellow note stuck to my desk. I was bending over to read it when my cell phone began to ring from the top drawer, the sound muffled and quiet.

I got it out and answered in a rush as soon as I recognized the number on the screen.

"Nolan?" I said, hardly able to believe it might be my missing brother.

"Chloe?" I head in Nolan's familiar voice.

"Nolan! Where are you?"

Sam heard me and came out of his office. His face grim, he grabbed my arm and pulled me back in to his office, slamming the door behind me. Taking the phone from my hand, he pressed the icon to put it on speaker and set it on my desk. Together, we heard Nolan say,

"I can't tell you. It isn't safe. I can't talk long. I just wanted to make sure you're okay."

"She's not, Nolan," Sam said, cutting in. "This is Sam, and she's been staying with me since men with guns broke into your place."

"Chloe," Nolan said, his voice pained. "I didn't mean for any of this to happen, I swear. Are you okay?"

"I'm fine, Nolan. Sam's keeping me safe."

Sam started to interrupt again. I elbowed him in the stomach and put my finger to my lips. He glared back at me. I knew he was itching to yell at Nolan, but for now I just wanted to talk to my brother.

"Nolan, tell me where you are so we can come get you," I begged.

"I can't. It's too dangerous. I don't want you to get hurt."

"Nolan, I can send Axel's men to get you. You can come in and Chloe will stay safe," Sam said, making a chopping motion at me with his hand when I tried to signal him to stay quiet.

"No, I have to go straight to Sergey."

"So you're not trying to steal from him?" I asked, relief washing through me.

"No!" Nolan said, sounding shocked at the idea.

"Is that what he thinks? Who told you that?"

"It doesn't matter," I said. "Why can't you just call him and have him pick you up?" I asked.

"I tried. I can't get through to him. He doesn't carry a cell and every time I call the phone rings through. I was supposed to drop what he wants at one of his card rooms downtown and when I got there I was jumped. I barely got away. The next time I tried the same thing happened. Now I don't know what to do."

"Nolan, can you write down a number?" Sam asked.

"Yeah," Nolan said, sullenly. He'd never liked being told what to do. I wondered how he could work for someone like Tsepov, a man who clearly expected to be obeyed.

Sam rattled off a number I recognized as Axel's cell. "Call Axel," he told Nolan. "If anyone can get you to Tsepov in one piece, it's Axel. Stop fucking around and get your ass out of play before these guys decide to come after Chloe. They're already looking at her as a way to get to you."

"You're keeping her safe?" Nolan asked, anxiety making his voice crack.

"I am. But she'll be safer when you give Tsepov what he wants and end this whole thing. Call Axel."

"I'll try," Nolan said.

"Did you write down the number?" Sam asked.

"Yeah, I've got it."

"Nolan," I said, cutting in. "Please, call Axel. Tsepov doesn't think you've done anything wrong. He just wants you to come back."

"You've talked to him?" Nolan asked, shock and fear tumbling together in his shaking voice.

"Sam and I saw him this morning. He called and asked for a meeting."

"Fuck! Fuck! Chloe, stay away from him. Stay away from all of this. Take her somewhere, Sam. Get her out of town until I can deal with this."

"I'm not going anywhere Nolan! Not until I know you're safe."

"Chloe, listen to me, you can't get near Tsepov or any of his people. I don't know who-"

The line went silent with an abrupt click and Nolan was gone. I cried out in anguished shock, shaking the phone as if that would bring him back on the line. Frantic, I redialed his number. Sam and I listened to it ring through to voicemail. Thinking faster than I was, Sam left the message, repeating Axel's number for Nolan along with an order to call him immediately.

I sank into my desk chair, adrenaline fading as quickly as it had struck, leaving me limp and depressed. Nolan had been so close, for the first time in days. Now he was gone again, and the way he'd been cut off left me fearing the worst.

"Sam," I said. "What do we do now?"

He wrapped his arms around me in a quick,

warm hug. "You're going to go make a cup of tea and go back to work. There's nothing we can do right now. At least you know Nolan is still on one piece. I'll give Axel an update. Let's hope Nolan calls him and this whole thing is over soon."

"Okay," I said.

I went back to my desk, work the last thing on my mind. I shuffled through the papers on my desk, trying to focus on what I'd planned to get done that afternoon. I was mostly useless, distracted by worry over Nolan and hoping that he would call Axel and end this whole mess. Sam came out of his office about an hour after Nolan called and stopped by my desk.

"I need to go out for a little while," he said. "Don't leave the building without checking in with Axel. This whole thing should be wrapping up soon. But I want you to stay where Axel's guy can keep an eye on you."

"Where is he?" I asked, looking around the empty executive suite.

"He's around," Sam answered. "We've locked down the building, so the only way in and out is the front door. We've got eyes on the front door and another guy making rounds. Axel wants your security visible to anyone out there who might think you're an easy target."

"Okay. I wasn't planning on leaving anyway," I said. "I have too much to do here. And so do you.

Where are you going?"

"I have a few errands to run," Sam said, his eyes shifting from mine. "And I want to stop by the Claremont site and check their progress. I may be back before five. If I'm not, call Axel to let him know you're leaving so his guys can follow you home. Axel had your car brought back yesterday after he took you to his office. It's in your normal spot."

"All right. Do you need me to pick anything up for dinner?"

"We'll figure it out later," Sam said. He started to lean down, as if to kiss me on the cheek, but someone walked by the outer office door, and he straightened, settling for a wink.

I smiled back and kept smiling even after Sam was long gone. It would take some time to figure out how to handle our new relationship in the office, but I couldn't help liking the easy domesticity of checking in and talking about what we'd have for dinner. I was trying to get my head back in my work. Sam had a proposal I needed to edit before he did his own final review. But the words kept swimming in front of my eyes.

When my phone rang, I jumped on it, glad for the interruption. It was Tim.

"Chloe? I wanted to check in and see if you heard anything yet. Has Nolan turned up?"

"Tim, I'm so glad you called. I heard from Nolan

a little while ago and he's okay."

"Where is he? Did you go get him?" Tim asked in an excited, anxious rush of words.

"No, but he said he's fine. This should all be resolved soon, so you don't need to worry."

"What you mean? Where is he? If you tell me where he is, I'll go get him," Tim offered.

"I don't know where he is exactly. It's so sweet of you to want to help, but this is actually really dangerous, Tim. I don't want you to get involved. I have a friend who's going to help Nolan, and he'll be fine."

"What you mean? Who's going to help him? Help him do what?"

Tim's anxiety was infectious. Lowering my voice, I said, "Nolan has something he needs to give Tsepov. He's been having a little trouble handing it over, that's why he was missing. My friend is going to help him and then everything will be fine."

Silence on the other end of the phone. Then, Tim said, "Well, if you're sure he's okay."

"I think he will be," I said. "I'm hoping that by the end of the day Nolan will be home. But I'll tell him to call you when he's back."

"Yeah, tell him to call me." I heard voices in the background on Tim's end of the phone. His voice faded away as he said goodbye and clicked off.

Checking the clock, I was annoyed to find that it was only two thirty. Up until Sam had left, the day felt as if it were on fast-forward, but once I was alone in the office time had begun to crawl. The stack of papers in front of me looked like a mountain, and all I really wanted to do was go home and taken a nap.

CHAPTER SEVEN
Sam

I paced in front of the Fountain of the Gods in the Forum Shops at Caesar's Palace, waiting for Dylan. I'd already checked Cartier, just in case, but I had a feeling Tiffany's would have what I wanted. I thought about making a quick run upstairs to Agent Provocateur to pick up something special for Chloe, but Dylan would be there any second, and I was too on edge to do anything but pace and wait.

I wasn't nervous about the prospect of walking into Tiffany's and picking out a ring. From the beginning, from the first moment I realized how I felt about Chloe, our relationship had been heading in this direction. She wasn't a woman I wanted to date; she was the woman I wanted to spend the rest of my life with. After three years of friendship and months of working up the nerve to make a move, I was done with waiting.

I didn't want to sneak around at work. It felt cheap, like we were hiding or making the way we felt about each other something to be ashamed of. But I knew Chloe would never be comfortable without a clear statement of our relationship. She'd never put it like that. She'd be appalled if she had any idea her fears about an office romance had led me here. But the ring wasn't about protecting her reputation. It was so much more than that.

It was a way to tell her, and everyone else, that this was forever. That she was forever. I'd never been more certain of anything in my life. So why were my hands shaking? Dylan showed up just before I walked past the fountain for what felt like the hundredth time, a knowing smirk on his face.

"Is this what I think it is?" he asked thumping me on the shoulder with a closed fist.

"If you think you're here to help me pick out an engagement ring for Chloe, then yeah, it is," I said, turning to lead the way into Tiffany's.

We were met by a woman in a trim navy suit. "May I help you, gentlemen?" she asked.

My throat stuck for a second. Clearing it, I managed to say, "I'd like to see your engagement rings."

I was treated to a brilliant, white smile before she led the way to the back of the store. Beside me, Dylan said, "I called it. I knew a year ago that you'd fall head over heels for that girl."

"Bullshit," I said. "You're only saying that because you wanted to ask her out, and I told you she was off limits."

"Well, you did me a favor. Because now I have Leigha." Lowering his voice so the saleswoman couldn't hear, he said, "Though I've been shopping at Harry Winston."

"No shit," I said, slowing down to put some distance between us and the saleswoman ahead. "You didn't say anything."

"I know. I would have but, I know it's fast. I thought you might tell me I was nuts," Dylan admitted shrugging his shoulders. I rolled my eyes.

"Man, I've known you for years. When you make a decision that's it. You know what you want. And she's perfect for you."

"I know. But I'm going to sit on the ring for a while. I don't think it's too soon, but Leigha will. I only just got her to agree to live with me. If I try to give her a ring she'll either jump on it, or run screaming."

"Good point," I said. "Though I'm pretty sure she'll say yes." I didn't know her that well, but it seemed obvious to me that Leigha was completely in love with my friend.

The saleswoman had moved behind the jewelry counter. Dylan and I stood side-by-side scanning the rings. I had an idea of what I wanted. Something classic but elegant. That's why I was at Tiffany's. And something… special. Something more than the traditional engagement ring. Big, but not too big. Too much ring would only embarrass Chloe. Cost wasn't the issue, I could afford anything they had in the store without breaking a sweat.

For Chloe, the perfect ring wasn't about size. It just had to be *her*. I looked over the rings, rejecting each one in turn. One was too big, the next two plain, another had too much going on. I was starting to worry I'd have to go somewhere else when I saw it. The ring that said *Chloe*.

A channel set band topped by a perfect round diamond, surrounded by circle of small, sparkling bead set diamonds, as if the central stone was wearing a crown. It was the perfect ring for a princess. Elegant, simple, yet not too understated.

"That one," I said pointing to the ring. "I'd like to see that one."

"An excellent choice," the saleswoman said. "The Tiffany Embrace. Romance and glamour. This one is two and a half carats. Is that the size you were looking for?" she asked, handing me the ring.

As soon as I held it, I knew it was the one. Two and a half carats was a lot of ring, but I didn't think it would be too much. And though I knew Chloe wouldn't want a ring that was over the top, there was no way I was getting her something small. Dylan looked over my shoulder as I turned the ring in the light.

"That looks like her," he said.

"I know, doesn't it?" I murmured, fascinated by the way the light caught the brilliant stones. Looking at it, feeling the weight of the cool platinum in my hand, I didn't want to wait. Part of me wanted to buy it and go straight back to the office. To slide it on Chloe's hand the second I saw her.

That wasn't going to happen. For one thing, I didn't want to propose while all the shit with her brother was going on. She already felt like everything was upside down and I hadn't helped by changing our relationship at the same time. So the actual proposal could wait. But I had to have the ring now.

I guessed the size. Unlike with her clothes, Chloe didn't have a spare ring handy I could check. But we could always get it adjusted later. While I was there, I bought the matching wedding band. Might as well. A wedding was, after all, the point of an engagement ring.

As the saleswoman walked away, my American Express Black card in her hand, Dylan said under his breath, "You just made her day." I had. I doubted she sold sixty thousand dollar rings every day.

"Do you have to get back to the office?" Dylan asked.

"Not necessarily," I said, "Why?"

"Since I'm here, I thought I'd stop upstairs and get something for Leigha."

"I could do that," I said.

With the ring burning a hole in my pocket, I wasn't sure it was a good idea to go straight back to the office. Chloe was under surveillance. She was about as safe as she could get outside of my house or Axel's safe room. I hadn't lied to her, I was still planning on stopping by the Claremont project a little later, but there was no reason I couldn't visit Agent Provocateur now, get Chloe something sexy, maybe a little naughty, and then go to the site.

I signed the credit card receipt with flourish, feeling like I'd done so much more than buy a ring. Even though Chloe didn't know it yet, I taken the first step toward the rest of our lives.

CHAPTER EIGHT
Chloe

At five o'clock I was ready to get the heck out of the office. Sam's project proposal was edited, and my inbox was at least moderately under control. I was also antsy and bored, a frustrating combination. The office was quiet, so no fires to put out there, and I hadn't heard anything about Nolan. I had my fingers crossed that he'd called Axel, but somehow I doubted it. Calling Axel for help was too simple and straightforward. So far nothing Nolan had done was simple and straightforward.

I, on the other hand, was more than happy to be simple and straightforward. Following Sam's directions, I picked up my phone and called Axel to let him know I was planning to leave the office. He sounded distracted, and said he hadn't heard from Nolan, but I should go ahead and leave. His guys would be following me.

I got my purse out of the drawer in my desk, shut down my computer, and turned off the lights, locking Sam's office door before I went. It was a little unnerving knowing that Axel's men were watching me when I couldn't see them. It was possible that they weren't that sneaky; I was just oblivious. That was fine with me, I didn't want to learn how to spot a tail, I just wanted all of this to be over.

Driving back to Sam's house, my mind drifted, and I realized that despite sleeping the night before, I was still exhausted. When my phone rang on the seat beside me, I jumped and swerved a little in my lane. Looking down, I saw Tim's name on the display. I sighed. I appreciated that he was worried about Nolan, but there was nothing he could do at this point but get in the way. Picking up the phone, I said,

"Hi Tim. Everything okay?"

"No. Everything is seriously not okay. You need to get here now." He was frantic, the words spilling out, high-pitched and tight, reminding me of his tension when Sam and I had met him in the coffee shop.

"Tim, calm down. Tell me what's happening."

"Nolan called me. He asked me to come get him. I did and… and Chloe he's in bad shape."

"Is he hurt? If he's hurt, take him to the hospital, Tim."

"I can't. I can't drive and before he passed out he made me promise not to call anyone, but I knew I had to call you. I need you to come here."

"Where are you?" I asked. Tim's obvious fear was leaking into me.

"I'll text it to you," Tim said. "Are you in the car? You sound like you're in the car."

His words shot out in staccato bursts and I raced to keep up. "I'm in the car," I said trying to reassure him. "I'm on my way, just send me the directions. I'll be there as soon as I can, and we'll figure out what to do. Is he bleeding? Does he need medical attention right now?"

"He's okay for now but get here fast, Chloe." The phone cut off, and I made a frustrated sound in my throat.

I stared at the road ahead, unseeing, as I tried to think. Before I could get my bearings on the meaning of Tim's call, my phone chimed with a text. An address and the words, 'Come quick!!!'. Tapping the address brought up the navigation app on my phone. It wasn't far, only a few miles from my current position. I made a split second decision and hit 'Start' on the app. A female voice directed me to get off the freeway at the next exit. Which was almost directly to my right.

Cars honked and swerved as I wrenched my steering wheel and barreled toward the exit, cutting off the sedan behind me and almost running a convertible off the road. I saw the driver give me the finger in my rearview, and another vehicle, a black SUV, follow the same path, pushing the convertible further off the road, missing the exit by only yards, blocked by the sedan I'd almost hit. *Crap.*

That was probably Axel's guys. I hadn't meant to lose them. If the sedan had swerved just a few feet in the other direction, they'd still be right behind me. I glanced down at the phone, planning to call Axel, but the map was a mess of squiggled lines and if I changed screen to place a call, I'd lose my bearings, even with the navigator giving me verbal directions.

A command to turn left tore my attention from the phone and back to the road. I swerved into my lane, only to make a hard right a minute later. I was lost without the map, leaving known commercial areas and heading into an industrial neighborhood filled with warehouses. What was Nolan doing here? And how had Tim found him?

I didn't have time to wonder. I was directed to make another turn, the navigation speaking over itself as it warned me of the next turn, then the next. After more than five minutes of driving, my heart pounding in my chest, my sweaty palms gripping the steering wheel, I pulled to a stop in front of a large square building. My car was the only one in the small parking lot.

Just as I was beginning to wonder if I was in the right place, getting ready to pick up my phone and call Axel to let him know where I was, the rusty door opened and Tim stuck his head out.

"Chloe," he called. "Hurry up, get in here. Nolan's asking for you."

I shoved my phone in my purse and jumped out of the car, racing to follow Tim into the building.

"Nolan," I yelled, looking everywhere for my brother. I didn't see him. I spun around to ask Tim where he was and slammed straight into Dog.

Dog grinned down at me, then looked over at Tim, who was sliding a bar across the door and locking it into place, shaking his head.

"That was too easy," Tim said, turning to face me. "You had me scared when you said Nolan was going to turn himself in to you. Not when we hadn't found him yet."

I backed away from Dog, a sick feeling in my stomach. Knowing the answer I was going to get, I asked, "Where's Nolan?" Dog laughed.

"Good question," he said. I kept moving away from him and felt around in my purse for my phone. I doubted they'd let me make a call, but maybe I could hit the right buttons by feel and get a call out anyway.

"He's not here?" I asked, still moving away from Dog. I'd figured that out already, but it didn't hurt to play dumb. Not that I was playing. I was here, wasn't I? Dumb enough to be caught in their trap. My eyes were locked on Dog's smug, grinning face. A mistake, I realized too late, when I backed directly into Tim.

His hands closed over my arms, wrenching them behind me. It was like the day before all over again, but this time I wasn't being taken to safety. This time I was in serious trouble. Tim threw my purse to the floor and held my wrists together with ease, securing them with something that cut into my skin. For a skinny guy, he was a lot stronger than he looked.

Dragging me backward by my hands, he pushed me down into a metal chair and said, "Hold her."

Dog's fingers closed over my shoulders, digging in, pressing me down into the chair. Tim took more of what I saw were zip ties and fastened my feet to the legs of the chair. The hard plastic cut into my ankles. I yanked against them anyway. They didn't give. Behind me, Dog cut through the tie on my wrists, giving me a moment of slack before he strapped my right wrist to the back of the chair with a speed that suggested he wasn't new to using zip ties as restraints.

For just a second, my left hand was free. Panicked, my breath coming in short gasps, I swung at Tim, catching him on the jaw.

"Bitch," he said, backhanding me across the mouth, driving my lip into my teeth. I tasted blood. He leaned in and I saw his glazed eyes, his pupils hugely dialated. Like the day Sam and I had met him in the coffee house, beads of sweat pearled on his forehead. Crap. Sam had said he was high that day. Was he high now, too? That couldn't be good.

None of this was good. I wished I'd called Axel from the car and taken the risk on getting lost without the map. I wished I hadn't gotten off on that exit so quickly, losing Axel's man behind me. I hadn't meant to. I hadn't meant any of this. I'd thought I was coming to get Nolan, not walking into a trap.

I licked the blood from my lip and looked at my captors. Tim shifted from one foot to the other, bouncing on the balls of his feet, unable to stay still, his eyes wide and gleeful. Dog just stood there, arms crossed over his chest, studying me.

"She'll be worth something when we're done with her," he said to Tim, who nodded. My blood turned to ice in my veins. "Get her phone and send the message."

Tim picked my purse up off the floor and pulled out my phone. It looked like he was tapping out a text. When he was done, he shoved the phone in his pocket.

"Let's see how long that takes," he said. Looking at me, he went on, "Now we find out how much Nolan loves his big sister."

"I thought you worked for Tsepov," I said to Dog. "Why are you with Tim? Why am I here?" I couldn't get the pieces to fit together in my mind. Since when was Tim connected to Dog? He'd told us about the poker room… he'd pointed us straight in Dog's direction, I realized, though at the time Tim had seemed clueless.

Dog snorted in amusement. Or disgust at my ignorance. I didn't care, I wanted to know what was going on.

"I do work for Sergey. Ungrateful asshole. I bust my ass for him, but I'm not full blooded like the rest of them. I'm the mutt of the family. The American," he said with a sneer, imitating Tsepov's accent. "I'm not useless to everyone. I've got buyers for that data Nolan's holding. And as soon as I get it, I'll be free of Tsepov. Your brother is going to make me rich." As an afterthought, he added, "And so are you."

Tim said, "You mean he's going to make *us* rich."

Dog shot him a dismissive look and agreed, "Sure, he's going to make us rich."

Tim didn't notice that his partner wasn't excited about his contribution. I didn't have good feelings about Tim's future with Dog. But that was Tim's problem. I was afraid of the answer, but I had to ask. "How am I going to make you rich? I don't have any money."

Dog laughed. Tim giggled, his eyes roving my body with a greedy gaze that felt like he could see right through my suit. Dog said, "We're going to sell you right along with the thumb drive of data we're taking from your brother. It's a lucky coincidence that our buyers for the data have a use for pretty young girls. The data is actually their side business. They're looking to get into competition with Tsepov. But their main deal is girls just like you. Sweet. Young. Lots of tits and ass. Easy prey. We'll sell you to them. And they'll sell you over and over until there's nothing left."

"Once we get the drive from Nolan, we should break her in," Tim said, staring at my breasts. Between my blouse and suit jacket, I was covered up, but under his eyes I felt naked. My skin crawled at the idea of either of them touching me. I closed my eyes and prayed Axel and Sam could find me before these men got what they wanted from Nolan and both of us disappeared forever.

"Maybe," Dog said, his own eyes lingering on my body. "I wouldn't mind getting a piece of that before we sell her. After the business is done with Nolan." Addressing me, he said, "I wasn't going to bother with you. But when I saw you the other night, I told Tim you could be useful. Our buyers are going to love you."

I jumped when my phone rang. Tim looked at it, then shrugged. "Her boss."

Sam. Axel must have called him. Or maybe he was just checking in. I wished with everything I was that I could answer the phone and hear Sam's voice. The ringing stopped. A few seconds later, the phone dinged with a voicemail. I wondered if I would ever get to hear it. The ringing started again almost immediately.

This time, Tim's eyes flared with excitement and he moved to answer it. Dog held his hand out and Tim put the phone in it, his lower lip pouting out in a sulk. Dog answered the call, saying, "Nolan. It's Dog. I have your pretty sister. You want to guess what I'm going to do to her if you don't bring me that drive in the next half hour?"

Dog snorted, then held the phone up in front of me. "Tell your brother you're still alive," he ordered.

"Nolan," I said, loudly enough that I was sure he could hear me. "Nolan, don't-"

I didn't get the rest out. Dog slapped me with his big, hard hand, striking my face right where my lip had split. Warm blood ran down my chin. Dog murmured into the phone in a menacing tone. I couldn't hear Nolan's response, but Dog grunted in annoyance and gave him the address of the warehouse. "Fine, then move fast. I'm getting bored, and little Chloe is tempting. Got me?" He hung up the phone, tossing it on a nearby table.

"He's coming?" Tim asked, bouncing again on his toes. Dog nodded.

"He says he's holed up outside Mountain Springs in a cabin or some shit. But he's on his way."

"Sweet." From the back pocket of his saggy jeans, Tim produced a knife in a black leather sheathe. He waved it in my direction. "Let's cut that suit off her and have a little fun while we wait."

Dog sighed and looked at me, shaking his head. "This guy is a pain in my ass." With no warning, he pulled a gun from the waistband of his jeans. The sound of the shot was deafening in the open space of the warehouse. I'd never heard a bullet in real life. They were quieter in the movies.

A perfect round hole appeared in the middle of Tim's forehead. For an endless moment he remained suspended in the air. Then he fell to the ground in a rush, like a balloon deflating all at once. I heard a scream coming from somewhere, sharp and high pitched. I looked around in a panic before I realized it was coming from me.

CHAPTER NINE
Sam

I was leaving the Forum Shops when the phone rang. Axel. Hoping he was calling to say they had Nolan, I picked up.

"Trouble," Axel said. "My guy following Chloe lost her. She pulled off 215 too fast for him to follow. Pushed a car off the road to do it and blocked the exit. He tried to pick her back up, but she's gone."

"Are you fucking kidding me?" I asked, losing my breath. "Why would she do that?"

"My guy said it looked like she answered a call right before she flipped. We're going to find her, Sam."

"Fuck, Axel. Where are you?"

"My office, for now."

"I'm coming to you," I said, hanging up. Fuck. What had I said about not leaving her alone until this was resolved? I'd promised her I was going to watch her back. Logic told me that Axel's men were a better safeguard than I was, considering their training. But no one was good enough if she managed to evade them. And if I'd been in the car with her, I'd know where she was.

The ring box in my pocket felt like it weighed a million pounds. Without Chloe, it meant nothing. Without Chloe, I had nothing. Driving on autopilot, I headed for Axel's office. I tried calling Chloe, but it went straight to voicemail. I told myself that this could all be fine.

She could have decided at the last minute to stop at the store. She could be in a spot with bad phone reception. I knew that was bullshit. Chloe knew she had to be careful, knew she was being followed by security. She never would have risked losing them unless something was wrong.

Axel met me at the door, his expression grave. "I've got every available man working the area where she got off 215. We'll find her."

I started to answer when Axel's phone rang. My heart lurched. He had more going on than Chloe, it could be about anything. But I needed it to be about my girl.

"What?" Axel barked into the phone. "Did they say where they had her?"

I waited, every muscle in my body frozen solid. Axel grabbed my arm and led me into his building, past the front desk and into an empty conference room, saying, "Hold on," he put the phone on speaker and set it on the table. "Sam is with me. Tell me exactly what happened."

It was Nolan, finally doing something right. "I should have called you before," he said, his words tumbling over each other. "I was going to. I swear. But you have to get to Chloe. Dog called, said he has her. He's the one who's been stopping me from getting to Sergey. I didn't know it was him."

"Nolan," Axel said in the unyielding tone I'd heard him use when he was running out of patience. "Where are they? Could you tell if Dog was alone?"

"In a warehouse. I'm sending you the address. Tim was there too. He texted me from Chloe's phone. They must have grabbed her-"

Axel cut him off. "Did they let her talk to you? Give you proof they have her other than using her phone?"

"I heard her. She was trying to tell me something, but I think he hit her. What do I do?"

"What's the time frame?" Axel demanded.

"I told him I was in Mountain Springs. So maybe another forty-five minutes before he thinks I could get there."

"Where are you now?"

For once since this whole mess began, Nolan stopped being a self-centered ass and played it clean. He gave Axel an address that was less than five minutes away. Axel told him the location of the offices and ordered him to come to us. "I'm going to put the phone down and get my men on this address. In case anything goes wrong, keep the line open until you're inside my office. Got me?"

"Yeah. Be there in a minute."

Axel straightened and picked up a land line. I waited, chest tight, hands fisted, while Axel relayed the address Nolan had texted to his men who'd been with Chloe. They went back and forth for a few minutes, talking in a short-hand I couldn't follow, while I stood there, feeling completely useless.

I was a smart guy. I was rich. I had connections. None of that was any use in getting Chloe back. I would have given every penny if Dog had asked, just for the promise of her safety. But he hadn't asked for money. What he wanted, only Nolan could give. I was going to fucking kill that little shit. After we got Chloe back.

Endless minutes later, the front door to Axel's building swung open to admit Chloe's little brother. I'd seen Nolan a few months ago when he'd picked Chloe up from work. He'd looked a hell of a lot better than than he did now.

His skin, normally the same warm gold as Chloe's, was pale, his eyes drawn and red. He looked like he hadn't slept or showered in days. At the sight of him, Axel hung up the phone.

"I've got men surrounding the building, but they can't get eyes on Chloe." Looking at me, he said, "There was a shot a few minutes ago, then a woman's scream. The healthy volume of the scream suggests that Chloe wasn't the one shot."

"She fucking better not have been," I growled at Nolan, who turned sheet white. He was the opposite of Chloe in almost every way. Tall and lean where she was petite and curvy, his hair dark and straight instead of light and wavy. But his eyes were hers and the sight of them so pained and afraid pulled at me even though I wanted to punch him.

"Can you get her out?" he asked Axel, ignoring me.

"Not without putting her at risk," Axel said. "There isn't a way in that provides any cover. Not that we can see. My guys can't get eyes on the floor, but they can see enough of the layout from the roof of the building next door to tell that it's an empty square. No back hallway or protected door. Someone has to go in."

"I'll go," I said. Axel shook his head at me.

"Sorry, Lancelot. Dog doesn't seem to have a problem shooting that weapon. And you're nothing but a threat to him. It has to be Nolan."

"Anything," Nolan said. "Just tell me how to get her out and I'll do it. This wasn't supposed to happen this way."

"What the fuck did you think would happen when you started working for the Russian mob?" I asked. Nolan stepped back and looked to Axel for help. When Axel only stared him down, Nolan studied his feet and said, "Not this. I was bored at my job and then I had a bad game. Tsepov was cool about it, let me work it off. And he had me doing some cool shit."

"Illegal shit," Axel clarified. Nolan shrugged.

"I guess. I didn't think about it coming back to Chloe, I swear."

I didn't say anything. There was no point. Nolan was too young, or too self-centered, to grasp how his actions had endangered Chloe. And now wasn't the time to explain it to him.

"Do you have the drive?" Axel asked. Nolan gave him a wary look. Axel put his hand out. "Stop fucking around."

Nolan dug his hand in the front pocket of his stained, ill-fitting jeans and pulled out a small, silver thumb drive. There was nothing remarkable about it from the outside, its value was in the information it contained. Axel plucked it out of his fingers, startling a "Hey!" from Nolan.

"Does Dog know what this looks like?" Nolan shook his head in a negative. Axel crossed the room and rummaged around in the drawer of the front desk. He returned with another drive, this one red with a thick black stripe around the cap. Plugging it into a nearby computer, he began dragging files onto it. Over his shoulder, he asked, "Does Dog know exactly what's supposed to be on the drive?"

Nolan shook his head. "No. As far as I know, only

Tsepov and I know. And I guess whoever Dog plans to sell it to. It's more-"

Axel held a hand up, cutting him off. "Don't want to know, kid. Seriously. Your boss is hanging back on this. He wants this drive, and he wants you back in the fold. The rest of us stay safe as long as we don't get in his way and we don't know what's on that drive. Got it?"

Nolan nodded. He watched the silver drive disappear into Axel's pocket with frightened eyes. Axel handed him the substitute.

"Don't worry kid, you'll get it back. I have no interest in pissing off Sergey Tsepov. But we get your sister out of there first."

"Yeah, okay. Just-" Nolan swallowed hard, his eyes still on the pocket where Axel had stashed the silver drive. "Don't lose that."

"I won't." Axel said. "Apparently, it's worth more than your life. Now pay attention. We're running out of time. This is how you're going to play this. And you're not going to fuck it up."

CHAPTER TEN
Chloe

Dog was getting agitated. Tim's body lay prone on the floor between us, a stream of drying blood across his face and the hole in his forehead the only things giving away that he was dead and not just passed out. I didn't know how much time had gone by since Nolan had called. Not an hour. More than twenty minutes. My eyes tracked Dog's gun, held tightly in his right hand, swinging with the motion of his arm as he paced the room.

Every so often, he'd stop, abruptly pivot and point the gun at Tim's body, making a 'POW' sound and laughing. Once, he'd turned it on me, but I'd squeezed my eyes shut and held my breath, not wanting to see my death coming. This must not have been entertaining enough for Dog because he didn't bother to do it again. I couldn't see, but I was pretty sure my wrists were bleeding from rubbing against the zip-ties. My cut lip throbbed. None of it really bothered me. It could be worse. Tim's wrists weren't bleeding. As long as I was alive to bleed, I was in good shape. No matter what happened.

I sucked in a breath, trying to force myself to calm down. One bout of hysteria a day was all I was allowing myself, even considering the stress of being a hostage, hanging out with a dead body, and having a gun pointed at me. Axel's guys would find me eventually. Nolan was on his way. Sam was out there somewhere. I had a good chance of getting out of this in one piece as long as I was smart.

I tried to relax, pulling slow, deep breaths in through my nose the way they taught in yoga class. I liked yoga when I bothered to go. I'd managed to calm down, at least a little, when the scrape of the door opening sent my heart rate flying all over again. A familiar dark head poked around the corner. Nolan. I sent up a silent prayer that he had a plan. And that if he did, it was better than whatever plan he'd used to get us in this mess in the first place.

Seeing Dog's gun swing around to point at the door, Nolan shouldered it open and came in, his hands held up in front of his face, palms out.

"Hey, you can put the gun down," he said, walking slowly toward Dog. "I'm here. No need for that. It's cool."

"You got it?" Dog asked, not lowering the gun.

"Yeah. Seriously, put the gun away," Nolan said, continuing to edge closer to me. When he caught sight of Tim, he stopped, all the blood draining from his face.

"Do what I tell you and you won't end up like Tim," Dog said. "Give me the drive."

Nolan continued to stare down at Tim's body. Whatever his plan had been when he'd entered, it was forgotten. The sight of his friend lying dead had buried him in shock. I needed him to wake up and get it together.

"Nolan," I said, keeping my voice barely above a whisper. It didn't matter, Dog was close enough to hear everything.

"Give it to me," Dog repeated. Nolan didn't seem to hear either of us. He looked up at Dog, his face twisted in confusion.

"You killed Tim?" he said, his eyes going from the hole in Tim's head to Dog's gun and back again. "You were friends. He trusted you. I didn't think you two were the one's behind all this, I thought it was Petr. But Tim never would have betrayed you."

Nolan might have gone on, but Dog laughed and dropped the gun to fire a shot into Tim's body. It flinched at the impact, but there was no more bleeding without a living heart to pump the blood. Nolan shrieked at the sound. I froze, my ears ringing, my vision blurring. It took me a few seconds to realize I was crying. Again. When this was all over, I was putting a moratorium on tears.

"Tim was a tweaker," Dog said, dismissing the dead boy on the floor. "He was useful when he brought you in. And getting that drive to me. But otherwise, he was a waste of time."

Nolan straightened his spine and stepped over Tim, moving to the side until he was blocking me from Dog.

"Sorry Chloe," he whispered when he was close enough to be heard.

"Don't get shot, Nol," I said. I wasn't going to tell him it was okay. It wasn't. But if we could both get out of this alive, I could be convinced to get over it.

"Let Chloe leave and I'll give you the drive," he said.

"You have it here?" Dog asked, his index finger tightening a fraction on the trigger.

"It's encrypted. You can't access the data without me."

Dog shrugged. "The buyer has a hacker, too. He can deal with it."

"Without the key, the data will erase itself," Nolan said quickly. "It's un-hackable."

"You're lying."

"Am I?" The thread of smugness in Nolan's voice must have convinced Dog that Nolan might be telling the truth. He'd put too much into this to risk blowing the whole thing over a hacker's trick he didn't understand.

"I can't let her go, man," Dog said, sounding almost apologetic. "There are too many people she can pull down on us. And I have a buyer for her, too. Just give me the key and I'll let you walk. That's the deal."

"And leave my sister with you?" Nolan asked, incredulous. "Let you sell her? Not going to happen."

"Then I'll shoot you and torture the key out of you." Dog angled the gun down and fired. Nolan flew back, landing against my legs, his head rolling to my knee. Blood welled through a hole in his jeans in the middle of his thigh, slowly at first, then in a thick stream, staining his jeans black.

"That's not too bad," Dog said, watching Nolan bleed. I whimpered, completely helpless as long as I was strapped to the chair. "You've got some time. Give me the key and the drive or I'll shoot you again."

"What good will that do?" Nolan asked, struggling to his feet. "If I'm dead you won't be able to access the drive."

"No, but I'll still have Chloe. She's worth more than you'd think."

Nolan managed to stand, wobbling a little, blood pooling around his injured leg.

"Fine," he said. "Get me a computer so I can decrypt this thing and I'll walk. You can have Chloe."

"Finally," Dog said. He edged across the room to a table in the corner I hadn't noticed before. A thin laptop rested on top, the screen closed. Dog picked it up, but Nolan stopped him.

"Leave it there," he said, limping across the

room. For the first time since I'd been tied to the chair, Dog turned his back on me. The first moment Dog, and his gun, were nowhere near my position, Nolan shouted, "Now!"

Everything happened at once. The door opened, and I heard a clanking sound, then something rolling. Before I could register that the cavalry might be here, there was a flash, the sound of a shot, and the room filled with smoke. It happened again less than a second later, a blinding flash, a bang and the smoke was even thicker.

I couldn't see anything. My ears were ringing. I thought I heard footsteps and shuffling where Nolan and Dog had been, but the smoke had me confused and I couldn't tell what was going on. Then I was moving, the chair I was in tilting back and rising in the air. I couldn't help it, I screamed. My brain was lagging behind my instincts, and my instincts were telling me to scream bloody murder. So I did.

At least until a hand slapped over my mouth and shut me up. My breath puffed in and out of my nose in short, panicked bursts. I heard another bang, and this time I could identify it as a bullet. Then two more in rapid succession and another scream, this one male. Nolan? I had no way to tell. I was being carried, still strapped to the chair.

Less than a minute later I was outside. Without the smoke obscuring my vision, I relaxed a little. At least now I could see what was going on. Then Sam was there, kneeling in front of me, cupping my face in his hands, his familiar blue eyes tight with fear and worry.

"I'm okay," I whispered. "I'm okay. I'm sorry, I was stupid. Tim said Nolan was hurt, and I was going to call Axel but I thought I had time and then I didn't. I'm sorry, Sam." I was babbling, not making any sense, but that didn't seem to matter.

Before Sam could speak, Axel crouched behind me and set to work freeing me from the chair. As he cut the plastic zip ties, he said,

"The whole point of a trap, Chloe, is that you don't know it's a trap until it's too late. You're not an operative, and you were worried about your brother. Let it go. You're safe, we got Nolan, and the bad guys are neutralized. Let's just count this as a win and move on, okay?"

"Axle's right, honey," Sam said. "Don't beat yourself up over it. All that matters is that you're safe."

Finally I was free. Before I could get up, Sam was there, lifting me into his arms, and tucking me against his chest. To Axel, he said, "Are we calling an ambulance or are you taking Nolan to the hospital?"

"Don't know. Have to make a quick call. Chloe should have someone look at those wrists. And she might need a stitch or two for that lip."

I looked at Sam, suddenly remembering the last few minutes before the smoke and the flashing light.

My eyes flicked to Axel, but he'd stepped away and was already talking on the phone.

"Sam, Nolan was shot. He was bleeding so much. Dog killed Tim. He shot him right in front of me." I was babbling, the memories rushing at me in staccato bursts. "Where's Nolan?" I asked.

Axel stepped back over to us. "We're taking Nolan to Tsepov," he said. I struggled against Sam's chest, wanting to stand up, but his arms tightened and he refused to put me down.

"He was shot," I said. "He needs to go to the hospital." Axel looked at me with somber eyes and shook his head.

"Nolan's fine. He took one in the thigh and another in the shoulder just after we got here. Bleeding's already slowing, doesn't look like he'll need surgery."

"You go to the hospital when you get shot," I said. Was I the only one who knew that? What was wrong with them? Axel shook his head again.

"Nolan's survival depends on his boss's goodwill, Chloe. An ER doctor will have to report gunshot wounds to the police and that will not make Tsepov happy. Do you understand? Tsepov has his own doctors. They'll take care of Nolan. Most important, Tsepov will be happy and your brother will remain alive. That's the best we can do for him."

I relaxed into Sam's chest and dropped my head to his shoulder, breaking eye contact with Axel. I got it. In a very real way, Nolan was out of my reach now.

He would always be my brother, and I would always love him. Always. But it was becoming clear he was no longer my responsibility. He'd tied himself to a man who created his own laws in a world I wouldn't enter. Not even for my brother.

I started to shiver in Sam's arms, suddenly cold and aware again of the throbbing pain in my lip and in my wrists. Sam rubbed the bottom of his chin against the top of my head in comfort, and said to Axel, "Can you get someone to drive us to the hospital? I'll call Daniel and have him pick us up."

"Yeah give me a second."

We stood there, watching as men in black combat gear and visored helmets left the smoky warehouse. Two of them carried Dog's body between them. Based on the bullet holes in Dog's chest, I assumed he was dead. Maybe that made me a bad person, but I was glad. Tim's body followed next. I had no idea what they were doing with them, and I didn't care. That was Axel's problem. Or maybe Tsepov's. It wasn't mine. Or Sam's.

Nolan came out last, half supported by one of Axel's men, limping, a rough bandage tied tightly around his thigh. He met my eyes, then looked away. I didn't know what to say to him, and I didn't have a chance to figure it out. He was gone a moment later, hustled into the same huge SUV that held Tim and Dog's bodies. It started up and pulled away from the warehouse, taking Nolan with it and out of my life, at least for now.

Sam carried me to another SUV, laying me gently in the back, before climbing in beside me. He pulled me into his arms, cradling me against his chest. He didn't say anything, just rested his cheek on the top of my head and held me, all the way to the hospital.

CHAPTER ELEVEN
Chloe

There were questions at the hospital. My injuries were more than a little suspect. Sam and I both assured the staff that everything was fine. Apparently a split lip that required two stitches plus badly abraded wrists were suspicious, but did not require a police report. We got more than our share of hard eyes from the nurses and two doctors who treated me. A plastic surgeon took care of my lip. There wasn't much they could do for my wrists aside from antibiotic ointment and bandages.

I was given a prescription for a painkiller which Daniel filled at the hospital pharmacy when he picked us up. Knowing it would be uncomfortable to eat anything, Sam asked him to stop and get me a chocolate milkshake which I used to wash down the pill. Less than an hour later, adrenaline gone and the pill in my bloodstream, I fell asleep. I woke the next morning, naked in bed, curled into Sam.

Sam babied me like crazy for the rest of the week. He refused to let me go into work, bringing home a shiny new laptop he said was set up to connect to my desktop at the office, in case something came up that couldn't wait. He didn't go in either, canceling all of his meetings and insisting on staying within arms reach. It was only a day and a half, so I didn't protest too much. Besides, after everything I'd been through, work didn't seem as important.

All I really wanted was to be with Sam. Well, I also wanted to see Nolan and assure myself that he was all right. My wish was not granted. The only way to see Nolan, who was recovering from his gunshot wounds, was to go to Tsepov. Sam refused to take me anywhere near the Russian, and I didn't argue that much. I wanted to see Nolan. But Sam was right. Our lives had intersected with Tsepov's too much in the past week, and no one wanted that trend to continue.

I did receive an enormous bouquet of red roses and white lilies with a handwritten note that read, *Be well. I'll look after your family as if he was my own. T*

It was not entirely reassuring. Sam wanted to throw out the flowers. I told him it was a waste, and gave them to Marte, who was more than happy to take them home. She fussed over both me and Sam, cooking our meals and baking treats, seemingly happy to have us to take care of. I was used to being the one who took care of everyone else, but I was enjoying it. I'd be back to my normal self soon enough.

For the first few days after Nolan was shot, Sam had a hard time letting me out of his sight. For my part, I wasn't too keen on being alone, so it worked out well. In the space of an hour I'd gone from a woman who'd never heard a gunshot in real life to one who saw a man take a bullet to the forehead and ended up covered in her brother's blood.

I slept a lot for a day or two. I think I needed that, to block out everything and relax with Sam. But by the end of the weekend, I was feeling much steadier, ready to get back to normal life. Or whatever would constitute the new normal, now that everything had changed between Sam and me.

Without asking me, Sam had hired people to clean up my apartment and pack what belongings I had that weren't damaged. They arrived that Saturday morning in a moving truck. Sam directed them to unload the boxes into an unused garage bay. Incredulous, I asked him,

"What is that? What are all these boxes?"

Hands in his pockets, Sam shrugged, a little sheepish as he said, "I had your things moved here. Was there any furniture you wanted from your apartment?"

"What?" Not an informative response, but I didn't have one of those yet. "What are you talking about? Did you move me out of my apartment without asking me?" I put my hands on my hips, but the flare of pain reminded me they didn't like being bent that way and I dropped my arms to my sides.

"You weren't going back there, were you?" Sam crossed his arms over his chest in challenge.

"Sam, you can't just move me out of my apartment without asking. And did you even ask Daniel how he feels?"

Sam stared at me. "Are you kidding? If you move out I think my dad would make me leave with you. Is that what you want? To go back to your apartment? Because I thought this was a really good," he said, his hand waving between us.

"It is, but, I just-" I broke off, trying to think. Did I want to go back to the apartment? No, I didn't. And not just because I couldn't forget seeing strangers break in, knowing they'd torn the place apart. I wanted to be here, with Sam. He watched me, his normally confident blue eyes anxious and uncertain. "I don't want to leave, Sam. I want to be with you. But isn't this too soon?"

"Is it? Chloe, it can't be too soon. We've spent every day together for three years, and for at least two of those you've been so much more than my assistant, you've been my best friend. I love you. You love me. So what else is there to wait for?"

"Nothing," I said. There was nothing else to wait for. Sam took me in his arms and kissed me. He pulled away before I was ready, and looked into my eyes, studying my face. Whatever it was he was looking for, he must've found it because he led me into the kitchen and lifted me to sit on the island.

"Stay there," he said. "Don't move, I'll be right back."

I waited, confused, the house empty but for the sounds of the movers going in and out of the garage in the distance. Sam was back a minute later, carrying something in his closed fist.

"I was going to wait," he said. "Do a big thing. But we don't need a big thing, we just need this."

I had no idea what he was talking about. He moved to stand in front of me. I spread my legs a little, stretching out my feet to catch him with my heels and tug him closer. He complied, moving forward until I could wrap my legs around him. I was thinking about stealing a kiss, at least until it looked down and saw a square turquoise box wrapped in a white ribbon.

"Open it," Sam said. I did, tugging on the ribbon until it fell away and lifting the top off of the pretty blue box. Inside was a smaller black velvet box. My heart clenched in my chest and I looked at Sam's face.

"Open it, Chloe," he whispered, tipping the blue box toward me so the velvet one slid out into my waiting hands.

With trembling fingers, I turned the box right side up and lifted the lid. Diamonds and platinum sparkled in the bright lights of the kitchen, blinding me with joy.

"Sam?" I asked, needing to hear him say it. Carefully, he pulled the ring from the box and took my left hand in his.

"Chloe Henson, you're my best friend, my partner, the most beautiful, strong, amazing, sexy woman I've ever known and the only woman I'll ever want by my side. I love you. Will you be my wife?" He held the ring just in front of my fingertip, waiting for my answer before sliding it on.

"Yes, yes I will." Sam slipped the ring on and we both stared at my hand. "I've loved you forever Sam," I said, unable to take my eyes off the ring he'd chosen for me. It was stunning. I couldn't have imagined anything that represented our love better. Though it was kind of big. But I knew Sam. He wouldn't have been able to help himself. It seemed he wanted everyone to know that I was his. Which was fine with me, because I wanted everyone to know, too.

He raised my hand to his lips and kissed it, saying, "I've loved you forever too, Chloe. It just took me a little longer to figure it out."

With that, he scooped me up off the kitchen counter and carried me down the hall, kicking our bedroom door shut behind us.

EPILOGUE

I watched the bride and groom spin around the dance floor, wide happy smiles on their faces, and leaned into Sam. After all the planning, it was wonderful to sit back and see Dylan and Leigha enjoy their wedding. Leigha and I had hit it off after that first dinner. About a week after we found Nolan, she'd called me to see if I wanted to get lunch. I'd said yes and together we had a blast.

I would've put up with her for Dylan's sake even if I hadn't liked her. But it made all of our lives so much easier once we discovered how well we got along. The only downside, and it was a small one, was that I got dragged into the wedding preparations. Leigha hadn't expected Dylan to propose. It was funny since she said she hadn't been surprised to see my engagement ring during that first lunch together. But as she'd pointed out, in his own way, Sam had been courting me for a long time.

She'd been thrilled about the idea of marrying Dylan, not so much about the wedding itself. Dylan had insisted on paying, since he was the one who wanted something big. And he'd hired the best wedding planner in Vegas to handle the details. I think the whole thing made Sam a little nervous. Sam was ready to get married, but like Leigha, he wasn't all about a huge production.

Though Dylan usually gave Leigha everything she wanted, in this his mind could not be changed. He wanted everyone to know that she was his. And since his profile wasn't exactly low, he couldn't just show that with a huge ring, he had to throw the biggest party in town.

Sam and I had tentatively set a date after Sam proposed, but hadn't gotten around to planning the details when Dylan gave Leigha her ring. It took about two weeks of exposure to the three ring circus Dylan had in mind before I brought up the wedding situation at dinner one night.

"I don't want a wedding," I'd said. Sam had looked up at me in shock. Echoing my frequent response to his crazy pronouncements, he'd said,

"What?"

Backpedaling, I explained, "No, no, I want to get married. I just don't want a 'wedding'." I made air quotes with my fingers. "Do we have to? I know part of the whole thing with Dylan and Leigha has to do with his job, and the Delecta, and what everyone expects from them. But I don't want all that. I just want to be your wife."

Sam let out a breath and relaxed. "Oh thank God. I don't want that either. I just want you in a beautiful dress, saying yes. And maybe some romantic candles and flowers and shit."

Daniel had broken in, saying, "That's all fine, but if you two think you're getting married without me there, you'd better think again."

Worried I'd hurt his feelings, I put my hand on his arm and assured him, "No, Daniel, not without you, that's not what I meant. And I'd want to invite our close friends. I just mean something fun and small without a lot of planning. Maybe we could go somewhere. Like a resort on a beach. I'd love to get married on the beach at sunset and then have a party. And everybody else could go home and we'd have our honeymoon. Simple."

And that's exactly what we'd done. Before Dylan and Leigha had even chosen a venue, Sam and I had picked an intimate, luxurious resort in the Caribbean that had a fantastically organized event planner. All I had to do was pick a dress and show up.

We were married less than six weeks after Sam put his ring on my finger and it was everything I'd dreamed. Though the wedding was low-key, I chose a dress fit for a princess, with a huge tulle skirt and a corset bodice studded with crystals and pearls. Sam had worn a midnight navy-blue tuxedo, so dark it was almost black. With his tousled blond hair and blue eyes he'd been devastatingly handsome.

Our guests had dressed as they pleased, some in bare feet and tropical dresses, some decked out for a formal affair. We didn't care. We had the sunset, and the beach, and each other. The only part that wasn't absolutely perfect was Nolan.

He wasn't at the wedding. We'd spoken over the phone, but I hadn't seen him since that day in the warehouse and I didn't know when I would. He seemed happy where he was, firmly ensconced in the middle of Tsepov's criminal empire. He said he missed me, but apparently not enough to break away and start over.

I tried not to take it personally. As Sam had pointed out, and Axel backed him up, getting away from Tsepov would be dangerous. As long as Nolan was happy enough working for the man, he was safer staying put even if it meant he couldn't see me. Since I wanted my brother alive more than I wanted him in my life, I tried to let it go.

Watching Dylan and Leigha dance, I slipped my hand into Sam's and gave it a squeeze. I was keeping a secret, and I thought he suspected. I wouldn't know for sure for another few days and I didn't want to create a distraction from Dylan and Leigha's big day. Sam was a smart guy. He was biding his time, waiting until I was ready. But I knew that he knew there was a reason I was drinking cider instead of champagne.

He leaned over to whisper in my ear, "This is a great party, but I'm so glad we ran away to get married."

I whispered back, "Me too."

In the back of the room I spotted something interesting and nudged Sam. "Look at that," I whispered. "Did you ever think you'd see that happen?"

Sam followed my eyes to the back of the dance floor where Axel stood with his date, tucked behind an enormous potted plant. She was almost hidden from the rest of the room, though she was tall and striking enough to stand out, with her flame red hair and pale creamy skin. He held her in his arms as if she were the most fragile, precious creature in the world, his lips grazing her cheekbones gently before landing on her mouth. His mouth took hers with carnal abandon, falling so deeply into the kiss I wondered if he had forgotten where he was.

Pretending to fan myself, I grinned at Sam and said, "Oh, how the mighty fall. Remember when he swore he'd never fall in love?" It hadn't been that long ago. In fact, he'd said it while laughing at Sam and Dylan as they'd debated some stupid detail about the wedding, promising that he would never be fool enough to get sucked in like his friends had. It was a good thing he hadn't known the havoc his redhead would wreak in his life the day her file landed on his desk. If he had, he probably would have run in the other direction and the rest of us would have missed the show.

Sam grinned back. "I told you, it was just a matter of time. Eventually, if we're lucky, love finds us all."

He stood and pulled me to my feet, drawing me out onto the dance floor where the rest of the guests were joining Dylan and Leigha in their celebration.

"Dance with me, sweet Chloe," he said.

I went to him with a smile, never happier than when I was in Sam Logan's arms.

THANK YOU

Thanks for reading The Courtship Maneuver!
I hope you enjoyed it!
* Don't Miss Out on New Releases, Free Stories and More!! Join my Readers Group!
* Reviews are a wonderful way for other readers to find books they'll like.
* Join my ARC Team. I love to give out advance copies to readers who like to read & review books before they're released.

Read on for a sneak peek of an all new serial by Alexa Wilder; The Temptation Trap!

ALEXA WILDER

In Case You Missed It…
The Wedding Rescue

She thinks she's not his type. He's determined to prove her wrong.

Leigha Carmichael is used to the quiet life. A junior accountant by day, she knows girls like her don't have exciting lives. She's smart, shy and her curvy body doesn't fit in among the beauty queens of Las Vegas.

Still reeling from her ex-boyfriend's betrayal, Leigha's sworn off all men. Except she has a huge problem, and only the right man can solve it.

The moment he sees her across a crowded bar, Dylan Kane knows he wants her. And Dylan Kane always gets what he wants. Especially when the object of his desire is sitting in his own casino. She's nothing like the skinny, overly made up women he's used to.

From her clear gray eyes to her luscious curves, Leigha is the real thing. Exactly the change of pace he's been looking for. And even better, she needs something from him. With the bargain he has in mind, they'll both get exactly what they want.

In the few days she's his, Dylan plans to take control of every delectable inch of Leigha's body. But when the weekend is over, will he be able to let her go?

Excerpt: The Wedding Rescue, Book One

I saw her across a crowded room. It's such a cliché, especially for me. I see beautiful women across crowded rooms all the time. The Delecta was my casino, and she was sitting at my bar.

It's hard to say what made me stop. She wasn't a showgirl or a model, and nothing like the tall, skinny, overly made up women I was accustomed to. No, she was something else. She was real.

When was the last time I'd had real? Real curves, generous enough to have her hips straining the seams of her navy blue dress. Real tits. Had to be. They were soft and full, even from a distance. They, too, strained against her dress. Mouthwatering. And her lips. A plump bow, ready to open for me. I had to see more.

Also by Alexa Wilder

Don't Miss Out on New Releases, Free Stories and More!!

Join Alexa's Readers Group!

AlexaWilder.com/readers-group/

Visit Alexa on Facebook:

Facebook.com/AuthorAlexaWilder

The Wedding Rescue

The Courtship Maneuver

The Stubborn Suitor

The Reckless Secret

The Temptation Trap

The Surprising Catch

ALEXA WILDER

SNEAK PEAK: THE TEMPTATION TRAP
Chapter One: *Axel*

Emma Wright was becoming a problem. She was supposed to be a job. An easy job. Get close to her, find evidence that she was selling confidential data to a competitor. Get paid a ton of money. How hard could it be? She was the head of Human Resources at a shipping company, not Mata Hari. This kind of thing was the bread and butter of Sinclair Security. I figured I'd take the meeting and pass off the case to one of my guys.

Then I got a good look at Emma Wright.

Fiery red hair, creamy skin, abundant curves, and clear blue eyes with a wicked glint. She was irresistible. Luscious, soft, and more than a handful in all the right places. The moment I saw her picture, I knew I'd be handling her myself.

Fucking the suspect wasn't usually my MO, but in this case I was prepared to make an exception. Normally, my approach was to get the evidence, give it to the client, close the case, and cash the check. Not with Emma.

Getting her into bed wasn't the hard part. Neither was pretending to be her lover. But Emma was tricky. She was smart. Funny. Gorgeous. And surprisingly kinky. Deliciously kinky. I'd never admit it, but it's possible I was taking my time on the case just to have an excuse to keep fucking her.

That, and it was harder than I'd expected to find what I was looking for. I kept waiting for her to slip. Everyone did, eventually. But so far, nothing. I hadn't caught her in even the tiniest lie. The client was getting restless, and I was starting to wonder if I was losing my touch.

I knew she was guilty. Most people were when it came down to it. I already knew what would happen in the end. Tears. Pleading. Excuses and justifications. None of that would matter to me. I'd taken the contract, and I would do my job. In the back of my mind, I was hoping it would last just a little longer. I hadn't yet had my fill of that lush body, and once I found the data Emma was smuggling out of Harper Shipping, she'd go to jail and our affair would be over.

Tonight my plan was to push her off balance, enough so she might make a mistake. Until now, I'd worked it out so that most of our dates were dinner at her house. More intimate and easier to search her place. When I did take her out somewhere, I chose places that were upscale, expensive, and not my usual style. I didn't need to be recognized as Axel Sinclair when I was pretending to be Adam Stewart. But tonight I'd picked a quiet, low-key Italian place around the corner from Emma's. I'd expected her to pout or act annoyed that I wasn't spending a few hundred dollars on her dinner. I should have known better.

Emma was relaxed, drinking her wine and digging into her fettuccine Alfredo. Watching the woman eat pasta was a torturous form of foreplay. When the creamy sauce hit her tongue, she sucked a stray noodle into her mouth with pursed lips, her eyes closed in rapture. I couldn't help but imagine her sucking me off with that same expression on her face.

She couldn't have cared less if she was in an exclusive restaurant surrounded by the best of Vegas society or a place like this one with paper napkins and a chalkboard menu on the wall. Emma enjoyed life however it came at her. I wondered if that would serve her well when she went to prison.

There was a chance she could avoid going to jail. Either way, I had to remind myself it wasn't my problem. My job was to find proof she was stealing and give that proof to her boss. What happened to her after that was between them. Most of the time the client didn't press charges. That kind of publicity was worse for business than the crime itself. But the owner and CEO of Harper Shipping had made his intentions clear. As soon as he could prove what she'd done, he was calling the police.

Knowing Emma, she'd get off with probation. She was smart enough to hire a good lawyer. And she'd be able to afford decent counsel. Somehow she'd managed to hide the money she was getting for the data she'd stolen. If my hackers couldn't find it, neither would the police. Which meant she had a tidy little nest egg somewhere out there, ready to provide a cushion when she fell.

Watching her wind pasta on her fork as she went on about a story a friend had told her, I found it hard to reconcile the woman before me with the liar I knew she was. I'd been in this game long enough to know that anyone could be a criminal, no matter how innocent they appeared on the surface. But Emma just didn't give me the guilty vibe. If I hadn't seen surveillance video of her rifling through secured files and copying them, then later handing them off to a competitor in a dark parking lot late at night, I would have sworn she wasn't the one they were looking for.

But I had seen it, seen her face clearly. Even had one of my guys check it. Video could be manufactured. This was real. On top of that, she treated her briefcase like it held the keys to Fort Knox. And she got jumpy whenever I brought up her job. In fact, it was the only time she acted oddly. Not guilty. Not exactly. But not her usual fun loving self.

All of it added together was more than enough

to convince me. Emma was guilty, and I would bring her down. A voice in the back of my head told me to find the evidence and close the case before I got in any deeper. But sitting across from her, my eyes glued to her lips as she sipped her wine, I knew it was already too late. I was in deep with Emma. And part of me, a part I'd thought long dead, hoped that somehow I'd find a way to prove her innocent.

About the Author

Alexa Wilder has been a sucker for romance since she found her first Harlequin at a hospital rummage sale when she was thirteen. While she loves all forms of the written word (so much that she occasionally gets caught reading the cereal box at breakfast), love stories have always been her favorite.

She lives in the southern U.S. with her husband, two sons, an assorted menagerie of pets, and spends most of her time dreaming up sexy, domineering heroes and the feisty, strong willed heroines who will send them reeling.

Made in the USA
Middletown, DE
13 May 2017